CW00457838

Sue J. Daniels was born in 1964 in North West London, she is from a strong mix of London's east end and Staffordshire heritage.

Since the age of six, Sue has harboured a deep love of reading and creative writing. She attributes this passion to her father, who taught her to read from the racing pages of his evening newspaper, even before she had started school.

The first book in her trilogy of novellas "The Salvaging of Sonny Chapman" won *Finalist* status in The Best Book Awards 2019 and The International Book Awards 2019. Both follow up books "The Restoration of Sonny Chapman" and "The Journals of Sonny Chapman" won *Finalist* status in The Best Book Awards 2020. The first in the series f DCI Rochelle Raven Crime Fiction, The Cubby Hole, also won *Finalist* status in the International Book Awards 2021.

Sue writes bravely, and with honesty in her heart.

To Jo
with best wishes
Sue

For my only brother, Tony…for always.

Sue J.Daniels

Glynis

Stoneface Publishing Audio

Lincoln, England.

A CIP catalogue record for this title is available from the British Library.

ISBN 978-1-8380356-0-0 (Paperback)
ISBN 978-1-8380356-1-7 (E-Book)

www.stonefacepublishingaudio.com
www.suejdaniels.com

First Published (2021)

Stoneface Publishing Audio.
Writing Rooms,
Main Road
Louth, Lincolnshire.
LN11 7TL

Acknowledgments

Again, my thanks go to the lovely team of supporters. To ACG Designs for the second book cover design in the DCI Rochelle Raven Series.

And again to Phillip Ward of yoda.coding.com an absolute oracle of internet knowledge and in making the promotion and online presence of my writing, so easy to negotiate.

To The Red Quill, editing and proofing service for whose continued honest structured critique, I seriously could not work without.

And a big thank you to the new addition of the production team, Deborah Balm, who is without doubt, an absolute asset to this series as she flawlessly narrates each book, ready for Audible, Audiobook availability.

To all of my beautiful, funny friends and family who know how long this dream and my retirement from reality has been simmering for. And, their love and continued support of my total weirdness and hilariously introverted personality.

Prologue

Love and Lucozade,

kept us safe,

kept us strong.

Memorable childhoods

of where we belong.

Some children though,

were born to wait.

Their memories bequeathed from

ancestral bitterness and hate.

To survive took guts,

keeping alive was key.

Hoping one day for escape,

To get away, to be free.

Chapter

1

Glynis Solomon came from a long line of angry, broken females. She had fought every day of her young life, to survive the regular outbursts of her violent, alcoholic mother, Marilyn.

Her Grandmother, Diane, seemed to hate her too, always telling her that was a scrounging bastard cuckoo. Glynis never knew what she meant by that but she knew it wasn't friendly. Diane told her she was weird because of her need to attempt to resuscitate dead animals.

This had come about because one morning after Marilyn had killed a mouse which had been digging in the hard cold white lard that Marilyn used in the chip pan, its little scratch marks clear to see. She had cut it clean in half with her husband's machete, which he kept by the back door in case of burglars, debt collectors or anybody looking for trouble.

After the mouse massacre, Marilyn had ordered her daughter to clean up the body. The first thing Glynis did was try to stick the mouse back together with some of her dads glue. Marilyn slapped the child hard and sent her to her room, laughing sinisterly as she did, mocking her and making fun of her intrinsic kindness.

Listen, is a perfectly descriptive anagram of silent. This is how she survived, it's what Glynis did most of the time. She listened to people, she listened with her ears and with her heart. Glynis had stopped talking at the age of two and a half and would back away from most people. She was so used to unfriendly people, always scared, always alone, trusting no one.

By ten years old, she'd learned to differentiate between those who were nice and those who were nasty, by the way in which the words rolled from a person's lips. Glynis had learned that to stay alive she needed to keep quiet, to be invisible and unheard.

Glynis's father, Raymond Solomon was a tall strong African man who had fallen on hard times after losing his job as a bus driver. He had only touched the little girl on the top of her leg by accident. That's what he had told the board when he was answering the case against him at the employment tribunal. They had dismissed him there and then.

He was by nature, a kind man but life had made him hard and lost. He was the only human being who had ever taken care of Glynis with any modicum of parenting, even though this meant that when he would read a story to her at night, his hand would find its way under the covers.

Glynis knew no different and completely accepted this as part of her father's love. He was for the most part, absent from her life as he spent much of his time taking, delivering and/or supplying drugs to local addicts.

Marilyn often kept Glynis away from school to wait on her and to clean up after her regular drunken nights, especially when her dad hadn't managed to find his way home after one of his drug fuelled binges. Regularly, her mother would use torturous behaviours against her, pinching her skin so hard that it left welts like red bruises and until little Glynis screamed out for her to stop.

One morning her mother who was still in bed screamed out to her. Glynis was putting out rubbish in addition to the already full wheelie bins. The dustbin operatives were trying to get her to talk to them but she quickly rushed inside, heart racing as she stood with her back to the closed door.

'Glynis, get up here now.'

'Make me some tea and toast and stop flirting with those men outside'. Her mother's words were like fiery darts, blaming, attacking and always painful, striking a never ending spike into her heart. She didn't know what her mother was saying to her.

Was she flirting? What did flirting mean. She had no idea but whatever it was, she would stop doing it.

Glynis nodded, with her head down, she hurried back downstairs, fighting back tears as they stung every cell in her throat.

A knock at the door made her jump and she nearly spilled the tray of tea and toast. Quietly placing the tray down on the kitchen worktop, she stood against the wall, staying very still, just as she'd been taught. The familiar sound of her mother's bedroom window opened and she heard her voice bellowing into the street below.

'Who is it and what do you want?'

'Hello Mrs Solomon, it's the truancy officer Mr Tony Williams. Your daughter Glynis has not been to school this week and we need to know where she is.' said the visitor, with all the authority he could muster.

'Well, she's not here, the little bastard is probably out causing trouble somewhere?' Marilyn snapped.

'Mrs Solomon, you are solely responsible for your child's attendance at school.' replied the officer.

As the conversation continued, Janette Sullivan, the other officer, was looking through the tall glass pane which was adjacent to the front door. She could see right into the hallway from which, the light shone into the filthy kitchen. She could have sworn she saw a flash of a child's bare legs running across the hallway.

Tony, the senior officer wrote a note and put it in the letter box and they left.

‘Glynis, get up here and bring whatever it is that idiot has posted through the door.’ shouted Marilyn from her bed.

While the shouting had been going on from the window, Glynis had crept into the downstairs toilet to hide. Picking up the note, she ran upstairs to give it to her mother.

Glynis held her head down, she waited while her mother read the note.

‘Right get yourself ready for school I’m not paying no fine or going to any prison, get out of here, now!’

Glynis was secretly happy to be going to school. Finding some school clothes from the unwashed pile by the back door, she tried to iron some life back into them. The heat from the iron accentuated the smell of unwashed clothes but she didn’t care, she was getting out and away from her horrible mother.

Her mother never used to be like this. Before the drink took over, she remembered her as a kind, loving mother. Even now, Glynis liked to sit outside, by or in the garage, because she felt nearer to how her mother used to be. She could close her eyes and remember doing sticking felt pictures with her. Her mum used to make them both laugh and giggle all the time. It made her so sad to have lost that part of her.

That afternoon, outside the school, a tired ten-year-old Glynis began walking home, dodging the name calling and sporadic punches and kicks from the other children. She didn't care, it was till better than being at home.

The house was empty when she arrived and she was relieved. She got herself some tinned soup and tinned potatoes heated them up together in a big pan. A previous next door neighbour who she'd known as Tilly, had intervened in fights between Glynis's parents a number of times, taking the child in for a few hours each time. She had shown her how to cook basic meals in case she needed to fend for herself when the drink had taken over her mother and father.

Tilly would have taken Glynis in permanently in a heartbeat, she was a beautiful child, she had fuzzy afro hair that needed plaiting or even braiding but it could be done. She thought how much better the child would feel without it being so crazy. She had the most unusual amber coloured eyes.

Marilyn would never have heard of that though, Glynis was too much of a cash point for her.

On the way back to the council office, Janette mentioned that she thought she'd seen a child in the house. Tony said that it wouldn't surprise him, the family were known for it and told Janette not to get too 'hung up' on it, and to speak with the child, well, you would be asking this child to testify against the only family she's ever known. And, do we really want to have that much paperwork.

Relatively new to the job, eagerly professional and conscientious, Janette decided to look into the family anyway. It wouldn't take her long and would do no harm, she thought to herself.

Chapter

2

Rochelle (Rocco) was leading the morning briefing in the Galaxy Missing Children's Unit. There was nothing too pressing, but all cases were still serious and the team were waiting for instruction and daily action required.

On the briefing board were;

Two missing children from warring, divorcing parents, a teenage runaway and a new series of possible trafficking of young girls. A child who had run away from her care home and was a repeat missing person (MIsPer).

Rocco was already tired, it was her first day back after two weeks leave. The whole family, her brother Conrad and his husband Martin, her ex-husband Mike and their son Albie, together with Niamh her sister, had been to Austria for some serious ski-ing. It had been the perfect get away, but Rocco hadn't been away from work for so long and it had been full on. She felt like she needed a further week off, just to sleep.

It was good to be back at work though, she loved her job. As always, she had missed her team and how they all worked together. Mags had, without being asked, cleaned her office while she had been away and a fresh batch of brownies awaited her in the big red biscuit box.

Biting into the crumbly chocolate delight, Rocco washed it down with a mouthful of milky latte.

'Oh my word, these are so delicious. Thank You. So, how are you Mags, have you done anything exciting while I've been away?'

'Well, as a matter of fact I have, I'm going on a date!' answered Maggie Seed, smiling.

'A date, oh fabulous, tell me more, tell me more.' Rocco asked, enthused now.

Sergeant Stacey Lord knocked on the glass and entered. Without question, she found her way straight to the biscuit box.

'Can I boss?' asked Stacey.

'Yes of course, help yourself, I can't eat them all myself.'

'Well I met him in Sainsbury's car park. I'd managed to lock my keys in my car and he just happened to see me in distress. He very quickly got into my car for me.'

‘Well, apart from the speed in which he broke into your car, which we will need to question, what‘s he like then, don’t stop there Mags?’ enquired Rocco.

‘Ha-ha, no he is a car mechanic, he said it was a trick of the trade. Anyway, it turns out that we went to the same school. Of course, it’s not there anymore and we’re both the same age. I guess I’ll find out the details on Wednesday at the Wheatsheaf.’

‘Mags will you be alright, you know, do you need me and Rocco to be in the pub, just in case?’ asked Stacey.

‘No I think I’ll be alright, I might even cancel yet.’

‘Well we’ll be there if you need us, these brownies are awesome Mags, thank you,’ said Stacey as she cheekily took another one, waving and smiling as she returned to the main office.

Mahesh (Hesh) Cole had recently passed his detectives exam and was being mentored. He was now working on several cases at the same time, as each day had its own range of different tasks and challenges. He was so full of energy and loved every waking moment of his job. He could be attending one MIsPer, analysing evidence connected to a potential kidnap or abduction, interviewing offenders and distressed parents or carrying out surveillance. It didn’t matter to him, he enjoyed all of it. He found it so extremely rewarding. He had seen Stacey leave Rocco’s office. He’d missed her being around. Knocking on the window he walked in, edging his way towards the tin of chocolate treat.

‘Oh they smell good.’ he said, with a cheeky grin.

‘Save me from myself Hesh, help yourself.’ said Rocco.

I just wanted to tell you boss, that I’m onto that Mr Lewis you briefed us about earlier. Turns out he *has* taken the daughter to annoy his wife. Apparently she wouldn’t let him have her over the Easter holidays and so he just took her. I’m on my way there now with a court order, to get her back home with her mother.’

‘Good work Hesh. How are things at home?’ asked Rocco with concern.

‘It’s okay Ma’am, she is with my father now and we are getting there. The kids aren’t taking her death well though.’ answered Hesh.

‘Hesh, if you don’t mind me chipping in here, there’s a brilliant book for kids who have lost a grandparent. I’ll have a look and see if I can get you a copy.’ said Mags in her usual compassionate and helpful way.

Rocco left Hesh talking with Mags and went out into the brand new sub department of the existing Galaxy unit. After the huge discovery of missing children at the disturbing Magpie House a year previously, it had become evident that without the expert assistance of her cybercrime team members, they would never have located them so quickly.

After a meeting with the top brass, one being her ex-lover Edward Trench (Trenchie). It had been decided that it was time to make more of Mark Walsh and Nate Bridges' expertise.

For them to take more of a strategic role, they needed to recruit two new members to assist them.

One of the newbies who had made it through their interviews was Ruth McCarthy, a very young at heart, thirty three year old. She had bright pink hair and preferred gothic clothing style, her simmering sexuality was hot enough to melt chocolate.

Both of her parents were mixed race and she jokingly called herself 'fourquarters' on account of the four different blends of ethnicity that ran through her blood. Her mother was half Pakistani and half Polish. Her father half Jamaican and half English. She spoke three languages and was highly articulate, competitive and hilarious, in equal measure.

She appeared to be a mythical, dark individual. An absolute throwback from the Camden Town movement from the 1970s and 80s. Never to judge a book by its cover, they soon found out that she wasn't as gothic as she dressed. She was completely the opposite, a true and vibrant romantic whose knowledge of the back end of the internet and dark web was immeasurable, she even surprised Nate with her quick fire interview answers.

She had soon become a much loved and important team member and repeatedly had them laughing at her speedy and often sarcastic comebacks.

Mark had been promoted to the role of Cyber Crime Manager for Missing Children and Young Peoples unit.

Still desperately in love with Rocco, he continued to hide it well. Relieved that she was back from her holiday. He hated her being away, hated not seeing, hearing her every day.

Rocco often caught him staring at her and there was a definite, simmering sexual tension between them as their eyes locked intermittently. This was ever more apparent since he had practically saved her life in a massive house raid where an organised crime gang of paedophiles were auctioning kidnapped children. It had been the worst case they had ever dealt with.

The other newbie who had been recruited, was fresh from university. He was George Black, he had found the interview very difficult as he wasn't used to being with people. To his surprise he was offered the position the same afternoon.

It had rained heavily as he started his first day in the Galaxy Unit. Mark had to remind him to dry himself off, handing him a towel.

He was twenty three and extremely proficient, especially with the important parts of the job.

But, he lacked common sense to the point where he readily admitted that he often couldn't remember where he'd parked his car or other trivia, as he put it. The new cybercrime section needed him and his methodical, obsessional way of doing things. He very quickly became an integral part of the section. He had no clear role, but it was in the making.

Mark and Nate were equally impressed at his utter commitment and the speed with which he was able to access, seek and find information on certain individuals in the depths of the dark web organised crime gangs. He would not always find the current target search but often, he'd come across terrorist cells and slave trade gangs, which they always passed across to the appropriate unit. They knew he wouldn't be with them for long.

Within nine months, three other departments had tried to poach him into their teams. He wanted to stay in the Galaxy team because he enjoyed it, they were like family to him.

Mags always looked after him as he was the youngest. He was quite enamoured with Mark Walsh. George hadn't come out as gay because he probably hadn't realised it himself. Everyone else had and they loved him for it.

He was a combination of awkwardness, super intelligence and pure innocence and most definitely a high functioning soul on a spectrum of disorders somewhere in a big mental health, medical book.

Chapter

3

The first internet quest didn't bring up much when Janette entered the names of Glynis, Marilyn or Raymond Solomon. On an internal search, however, Marilyn's friends' list on her Facebook account offered more. She found a whole world of people who were heavily into drugs and alcohol. There were posts about kids being burdens and just a myriad of disparaging terms about parenting as a whole.

A woman called Tilly Shepherd had left some rather honest but critical remarks on some of Marilyn's posts. Her profile revealed sufficient information for her to believe that she might be able to throw some light on the fact that this child was possibly a safeguarding issue or a child at risk

Previous posts on her status mentioned things like **'Another child who will slip through the net as a statistic of children killed by their parents'.**

None of this sat right with Janette and knowing there was something significantly wrong with the situation, she was on to it like a blood hound. She didn't care what Mr Williams thought about extra paperwork, he was due to retire in a few months. He didn't really care about these kids anymore, but she did. She would rather be wrong and reprimanded than right and allow this child to suffer.

It was over and above the office protocol but she felt that she had to speak to this woman, she had to follow up on her gut feeling.

The phone call was over quick and Janette knew she was going to get the information she needed.

'Okay I'll meet you outside the library at 6 o'clock.' said Tilly Shepherd.

'Thank you, see you later'. said Janette as she thought to herself, just how wrong this was in terms of boundaries and protocol.

The street by the library was quiet. Janette recognised Tilly Shepherd from her picture on Facebook as she walked towards her. She introduced herself and suggested that they go and talk in the garden of a nearby pub.

'So what's this all about then, you've told me you work for the council, is that little girl okay?' said Tilly, a sense of panic in her voice. As she put down the two soft drinks.

'Look, I do work for the council but I'm not here in a work capacity, I just wonder what you can tell me, what do you know about the little girl called Glynis and how she is living?' said Janette with compassion, recognising the fear and worry in this woman's eyes.

Tilly shifted in her seat and sat up straight, she looked at Janette questioningly for a minute or two and then related how she knew the family from when she used to live next door. She explained how she often heard the child screaming throughout the day. How she had complained many times to the social services but that nothing ever seemed to get done.

'I only go on Facebook to try and see photos of Glynis but that bitch, she couldn't care less about her.

All these posts you normally see of parents gushing about their children you know the kind; "These are my world" "I love this kid", never, ever does she post stuff about Glynis, unless it's hateful. You only ever see pictures of that witch.' said Tilly, clearly angry at the lack of safeguarding response and knowing the danger this child was in.

Once back in the office, Janette got straight onto the safeguarding office at the local authority. She was told to enter the same paperwork to the court for an emergency protection order to be served on the parents within a forty eight hour period.

Methodically, once this was complete, she then contacted Children's Services to submit a referral citing that the child needed immediate protection and that urgent action needed to be taken.

Grabbing her coat and bag, Janette left her office and made her way to the school. Much to her surprise, she found Glynis in the playground on her own.

She walked directly over and sat on the low wall next to her.

Janette took in her unkempt, dirty looking hair and the smell of the child's unwashed clothes.

'Hello Glynis, my name is Janette and I am here to take care of you. I'm on your side okay.'

The child didn't answer, she just looked at the woman with her beautiful, burnt orange eyes.

The headmistress, Morwena Clarke, met them in the playground and ushered them to her office.

Glynis sat in the chair furthest away from everyone else and kept her head down. She listened intently as they discussed her and how she needed to be safeguarded until the parents and the home had been investigated properly. Janette was leaving no stone unturned as she systematically went through each concern. The reasonable grounds from which she believed that the child was suffering.

With some team effort and lots of calls later, an emergency protection order was granted and Glynis was going to be taken to a care home for a short period of time while they worked out a suitable placement with foster parents.

The rain continued to hammer down when Janette and Glynis arrived at the Heartsholme Children's Home.

Laughing together, they had to run in with their coats over their heads and even then, they were soaked through.

After the care home manager Cynthia smiled, moaned about the weather for a while and handed them a fresh dry towel each, she tried to make conversation with the girl.

She showed Glynis to her room, Janette was permitted to accompany them and stay with her for a while as she found her bearings and settled in.

Although she didn't speak, Janette could see that she was listening intently to every word she said. So she patiently went through the contents of the room with her. It was freshly painted, two lime and two white walls.

The bedding was also lime and a white and big emerald green rug monopolised most of the floor. There was a desk and chair, a wardrobe, small sink in the corner with a vanity unit built in and a divan bed. Glynis had never seen anything like it. Janette could have sworn she saw a smile on the little girls face.

On the way to collect Glynis, Janette had popped into her office. She knew there were some donated toys that had been handed in and she wanted to give the big brown bear to Glynis, so she had something to cuddle, something to make her feel safe and loved.

The first night in the children's home, Glynis sat on the bed. She couldn't stop looking all around her. This was her room. She tentatively laid down, not daring to actually get in to the fresh clean sheets. She could barely remember ever having such luxury, although somewhere deep in her memory she did have flashbacks of her mum tucking her into clean sheets and kissing her forehead.

In the semi darkness, she took in the details of the room that she was now meant to call home and carefully processed each item, the patterns on the ceiling and the woodgrain in the vanity unit, the vibrant colours and even the fibres on the rug.

Doing this helped her to shut out the noise from the other children. There was mayhem outside as one particular girl was screaming at the support worker at the main reception. She had been stood there shouting and defending another child, when Glynis came running in from the rain with the Social Worker Janette.

The girl was Layla Anderson, their eyes fixed on each other as if there was some kind of recognition.

Up until now, barely coping psychologically, Glynis had been dragged through her childhood, she was confused and afraid as her silent, subconscious rage simmered. Keeping herself tightly locked, like a coiled spring, observing all around her, but never speaking.

That was until Layla took a special interest in her.

Layla was beautiful, she was from a blend of Swedish and Australian parents. Her mother Pippa Anderson had come to England in her late teens on a gap year, and stayed until she was thirty. When she decided to return to her native Australia, Layla steadfastly refused to leave her home and her friends and so her mother had no choice but to put her into care.

Layla could see that Glynis was a frightened and nervous child. She didn't push her, but every day when she saw her in the day room or the dinner hall, she would just sit with her, just next to her, near enough for Glynis to know that she was there. She never spoke, just sat and waited.

One afternoon, Jacksy, a very irritating bully who Layla had already beaten to a pulp on more than one occasion, decided it would be a particularly good idea to push his trousered groin and gyrate it into a sitting Glynis's face.

On seeing him assaulting the girl and laughing like a hyena at himself, Layla sprang up from her chair and was across the room in seconds, grabbing the boy's hair from behind, she slammed him to the ground before he had a chance to say a word or defend himself. He got up and ran off out into the garden crying like a baby.

Gently offering her hand out towards Glynis, their eyes locked again, just like on the first day they'd met in the reception.

Janette visited regularly and within six months she had arranged for her to try spending some time in a foster home, just to see if she could adjust to living with a family, in the hope that she might one day be adopted.

Her first potential long term placement didn't go well. It was with William (Billy) and Jessica Coleman.

One Thursday afternoon her foster father 'Billy' had killed a rat on their farm. A big old rodent, he had been after it for a while. He'd taken its head clean off with his grafter spade, burying it behind the tractor shed. He didn't notice Glynis watching, he just saw her little red pumps racing past where he'd just come from.

Intrigued, it was his turn to hide in the shadows. He watched as this child, his new foster daughter, started digging with her tiny bare hands.

Finding the severed head of the dead rat, she gently lifted it out of the ground. Holding it in her hands, smiling and talking to it like an old friend, no thought whatsoever for the smell of death, blood and gore that that spewed out of its scrawny neck all over her already filthy hands. She desperately tried to reconnect its dismembered head back onto its body.

'No, no Glynis, put it down, it's full of disease, please put it down right now!' pleaded Billy.

Shocked at being caught with the rat and blood on her hands, Glynis dropped the rats head, she ran out of the yard and kept running.

Billy chased after her but soon lost sight of any trace of her and even back at the farmhouse, she was nowhere to be found. They decided to leave her for an while, sure that she would come back on her own once she had calmed down.

Darkness started to descend on the farm and Jessica Coleman called the police, she explained what had happened and that Glynis had been gone for a couple of hours.

The police officer who took the call was called DC Hesh Cole, he gave her a crime number and told her that he and his colleague would come out to the farm to take a statement in the next hour or so and for them not to worry.

Billy then made the call to Janette and told her what had happened.

He said he felt that the relationship had already broken down and feared for the influence she might have on the other children. What sort of child would do such a thing he told her? What sort of life had she really come from, was she insane? He told her that he and Jessica had decided that they didn't feel they could help this child, she was far beyond the level of any help they could give.

Chapter

4

After he'd received a call. Hesh shared the information about a missing child who had run away from her foster home. Rocco read through the alert and tasked Hesh and Stacey to go and speak to the foster parents again and to knock at the neighbouring properties. She wanted to be kept informed of every single step.

Child Rescue Alert

***Glynis Solomon**
***Afro Hair**
***Amber eyes**
***Mixed Race with freckles**
***Female – small build**
***10 Years old**
***Ran away from her placement foster home on Aldrich Farm, Coleman Estate, Callachen Heights.**

’You can drive Stace, I’m not feeling one hundred percent today and not even sure my responses will be quick enough, should they need to be.’

‘Yes of course, no problem mate. You know I love driving.’ replied Stacey.

They drove firstly to take a statement from Billy and Jessica Coleman. Pulling into the drive they were met by three young children and four dogs, which consisted of three terriers and a huge mastiff looking animal.

‘Come on in, they are all friendly, the children, not so much.’ joked Billy.

‘Thank you Mr Coleman.’ replied Stacey as Hesh played with the dogs and chatted with the young children.

I’m Sergeant Stacey Lord and this is my Colleague Detective Cole. We just need to ask some questions about your foster child and what happened before she ran away, if that’s okay with you?’ asked Stacey.

They went into the house, Billy took them into their front lounge where he said, it was kept nice for visitors.

Billy couldn’t contain his anguish as he explained what had happened with the rat and the digging it up.

‘I mean, seriously, I’ve never seen anything like it. That kid must be so damaged to be doing that sort of thing. I feel for her, I really do, but we don’t have the skills to deal with that sort of shit.’ said Billy, regretfully.

‘It’s okay Mr Coleman, it’s not your fault. These children are prone to disappearing, they have never had any guidance or know any different. She is in the system and we will find her and find out exactly what’s going on.’

‘Would you mind just letting us know that she is safe, we do care you know. We just can’t deal with her. She was a funny little thing. Never spoke, didn’t play with the other kids. She just sat on her own in the corner, always watching, observing, keeping herself safe, no doubt.’ asked Billy.

‘Of course we will let you know Billy. Don’t worry.’

The statement was complete and Hesh took a call on his radio.

‘We need to go now Stacey, they think they’ve found the girl.’ said Hesh urgently.

‘Thanks for your time. We’ll see ourselves out.’ said Stacey as they left quickly.

Chapter

5

Graveyards had never bothered Glynis, they were in fact, her favourite place. The dead didn't seem to trouble her either. She could escape bullies and the nastiness of people who were unkind to her in a grave yard. She loved to sit and watch the owls swoop to the ground as they fired suddenly down, a ghostly arrow, spearing an unsuspecting mouse or frog.

Tonight she felt she needed to be here, she had seen a funeral taking place the day before when Billy and Jessica had wanted to drive her into town to buy new clothes. The fog somehow looked translucent and beautiful in the light from the street lamp, as it cast a halo of mist above the gravestones.

Silent tears fell onto the cold stone and she knew she needed to find comfort. She needed to be on the grave of an older woman, someone she could feel close to, someone who reminded her of the mum she remembered. As terrible as it was at times, Glynis missed her home and even her mum.

The ground was soft as she started to dig at the grave, methodically she moved a small piece at a time. She had no idea what she was looking for, it was always the same. Digging and digging until she could dig no more but it made her feel useful. It was like she was searching for something, but she never knew what.

Layla told Janette and Rocco that she thought she might know where Glynis had gone. She told them about how she had seen the girl drawing a picture of a funeral procession she had seen with her foster parents. The churchyard sign that she had drawn had said Marsh Lane Cemetery, and there was only one of those in the area.

Joan and Matt Moriarty hadn't long lost their mother. Visiting her grave was their only real connection. Taking flowers and spending time at Marsh Lane Cemetery had become a daily routine for them.

When they'd found a young girl digging into their mothers remains, it was more than they could take and Joan instantly took her mobile phone from her pocket, hitting the emergency services button.

'Police please, there's someone at our mothers grave, it is a child and she is desecrating, vandalising it. It's disgusting. Please come and stop her.' screamed the distressed woman.

When the police arrived at cemetery, Stacey's heart melted as she saw the young girl laying on a newly laid grave. There were flowers all around her and two wreaths at her feet.

Stacey started to move closer towards Glynis, she could see the glistening moisture in her eyes, the soil from the digging caked on her face and hands. She looked like a wild, wounded animal.

In what seemed like seconds but was more likely fifteen minutes, the light from Hesh's torch encircled the child in a halo of light. Stacey moved in more quickly towards her and carefully took her filthy hand.

'Hey, come on now, this isn't a good place to be playing is it, let alone digging. Let's get you cleaned up and see if we can find you something good to eat eh?'

Glynis didn't resist. She liked this lady, she was kind, she had a nice face and smiled a lot. Hesh drove them back to the station in silence. They went straight to one of the 'soft' interview rooms. There was a bathroom with a shower, hand basin and toilet just off of the interview room which was most often used for working with victims of sexual assault and rape cases.

Stacey showed her to the bathroom and asked Mags to help her by making sure she didn't run, while she went to get Rocco and find some fresh clothes from their store. They always kept children's clothes, it had been Mags's idea.

The Galaxy Team often picked up missing children, many of whom were either soaking wet or filthy from their ordeals. It was nothing new to any of them.

Rocco lifted her head up from her computer as Stacey gave a quick knock on the glass and walked straight in.

'What's up?' asked Rocco.

'We've found the child, she's getting cleaned up right now. I'll get her something to eat and then is it okay if we interview her together?' answered Stacey.

'Yes of course, where's Hesh?' asked Rocco.

'Well, after what's just happened at the cemetery, I don't think he's doing too well after losing his mum and all that. Probably best that you send him home actually?' answered Stacey tentatively.

'We'll need an appropriate adult.' said Rocco.

'That's okay, the foster parents gave me the girls' social safeguarding workers number.' replied Stacey.

Stacey went back to the interview room and took Glynis down to the canteen with Mags, she couldn't be left alone. Glynis got through a full English breakfast, four slices of bread, two glasses of milk and a chocolate bar. Neither Stacey or Mags could believe how such a small child could eat so much. They both smiled at her, she smiled back still not speaking to either of them.

What was planned as a normal interview, didn't go very well because Glynis wouldn't talk to anyone. She sat with her head looking down. Janette took her back to Heartsholme children's centre, talking to her all the time but getting no reply.

She knew that the child was listening because of the concentration in her eyes.

Rocco had told him to go home but Hesh left them to do the interview. Going back to his desk he called the job in to social services. He knew that a lengthy Strategy Discussion would now need to take place between the police, social services, health and the child's school. All information on children that went missing had to be shared among every agency involved, it was often their only way of finding them. One tiny bit of information could lead them down an avenue that they had no reason to look otherwise.

Rocco was intrigued by the child. She arranged for more of a wraparound type of care. After speaking more in depth with Janette, who seemed to be more in tune with the girl, they arranged for a TAC (Team around the Child) meeting at her school. The team was then put in place to give her everything she needed, to be able to fit in at school, as well as the care home. She would soon be moving up to a new school and a whole new set of friends and new beginnings. She was determined not to let this girl slip through the net.

Chapter 6

Lukas Baltakis felt rough. His years of drinking Lithuanian Gold Vodka had taken its toll on his liver, and it hurt. He had his life etched upon his oily, acne scarred face.

Evidence of the years in the sun, mixed with the alcohol abuse, filled every wrinkled and weathered crevice.

His next consignment order was due to be shipped back to Lithuania in one months' time, and he didn't have quite enough stock. This order was for younger girls and he intended to get his men to find them for him.

Four years previously Lukas had no choice but to lay low. Two over efficient border officials had found and seized twenty three teenage girls from inside a hidden sealed compartment of a refrigeration lorry. He had escaped onto another lorry bound for France. He was surreptitiously dropped off along the Route nationale 20 (N20) in a place called Latour – de – Carol. From there he had found his way down to the end of the Canal de Midi not too far from Narbonne.

After a couple of nights of sleeping in a barn, he came upon a derelict house on the canal. This became his home for four months.

He could never understand why such a beautiful house would be left empty. The walls were made from original horsehair plaster. He had seen his grandfather and uncles mixing the lime, sand, plaster and horsehair in the family home when he was a small child. His memory triggered him to a day when he had been sent to cut the horses tail hair for the mix. The horse was a grumpy old chestnut mare and she had kicked him clean in the stomach, knocking him to the ground. Crying out, the men rushed to help him, calling for a doctor immediately. He had severe bruising, but he was okay. He had been frightened of horses ever since.

In the canal house, there was a cellar, tiled with a mosaic patter of black, clay pink and white ceramic tiles. It was dusty, but overall the whole house was in good condition. It just required some love and care and a some gentle renovation to modernise it.

Lukas fished everyday with an old rod and line that he had found in an outhouse, he'd fished every weekend as a boy and it made him feel safe and grounded.

It was like a Mary Celeste house. So much of somebody's life had been left in the perfect hideout.

He had been thinking about finding a place to retire to, a place that would take him away from the organised criminality and where he could never be found. He decided that he had found his place. He thought that his first choice would have always been Poland but he knew he would be found there and drawn in again. No, this place had captured his heart. The French easy way of life suited him. He spoke a little of the language, enough to purchase what he needed at the shop and to pass pleasantries.

Now as he waited for news from his procurement team, as he liked to call them. He laid his head back on his easy chair and dreamed of the whitewashed walls and copper pans that he would have in his kitchen. The piece of land where he longed to grow his own vegetables, keep chickens and bees for honey. The simplicity of freedom was his way out, his dream.

The border forces had found twenty three girls in one haul. The chance of getting the girls through far outweighed the risk of getting caught. But there were at least another forty girls that did get through and for which he received a hefty sum of money. It was this pay out that had enabled him to purchase the derelict house. He already had two French men working on the basic renovations such as a new water supply and drainage and installation of an oil fired central heating system.

It was his plan to move there as soon as this job was over, it was definitely going to be his last job and the money he would get paid for these young girls would easily be enough to see him through to his demise.

He wanted nothing more now than peace, to live his life simply, in the land of latte and lavender.

Chapter 7

Glynis had found a new spot in the local graveyard, it was between two very important looking graves. Both had high turrets and those coloured kind of frosted glass chippings. One had green and the other one had white, she loved the way they sparkled when the sunlight caught them at just the right angle. It made her wonder if stars would shine in the same way if she could ever get close enough to them.

She laid down in between the two graves, there was just enough room for her, a perfect fit. Looking up at the sky, through the trees, she wondered what was going to happen to her now.

Memories started to flood in and out of her brain, it was like a film before her, her early childhood, her father, her mother and another woman who she kept seeing in her mind. Was it Diane, her scary grandmother, now she was horrible to her, always making fun of her. She did bring her sweets sometimes, she said they were to shut her up.

Glynis didn't understand what had changed in her life, what had made everything go so wrong.

Maybe it was her dad losing his job. Whatever it was, she was free of it, at least for a while. They would probably send her back at some point.

She didn't speak because she never really knew what to say to anyone without getting told off, it had been easier for her to just keep quiet. The beatings had seemed to be less if she kept her mouth shut.

Glynis drifted off into a daydream where she was in the sea, one minute she was swimming and the next she was being pulled down, under the deep, deep water.

She awoke with a start and thought she was in another world. A soft mist had descended on the grave yard, she thought it was truly beautiful, smiling to herself, taking it all in.

Glynis could have stayed there in that graveyard forever, but she knew she had to go, she had to go back to the children's home or she would be missed. That was new in itself for her, at least people cared about her now.

Chapter 8

Trenchie (DCSI Edward Trenchard) was still hopelessly in love with Rocco and made her fully aware of that at every opportunity. He was always trying to rebuild their old affair in the hope that they might one day start again, but properly, get married and move in together.

There was no way Rocco would ever leave the Mill she lived in, her parents had put far too much work into that for her to sell it and she would never dishonour their memory by selling or leaving it, not for anyone or anything.

Since Albie had been taken from her and her family so mercilessly by a paedophile gang a couple of years before. Nearly losing him forever had changed her focus. She didn't want a relationship, she just wanted to do her job to the best of her ability and to keep her son and family safe from harm.

In his own way, Trenchie knew this. He couldn't stop thinking about her all the time and was sure that she had absolutely no idea what effect she had on men.

He thought about her beautiful long dark hair and the way she seemed to glide through the office as if floating. How she laughed with her colleagues. She always looked immaculate and her scent was beautifully unforgettable. He daydreamed as he looked longingly out of his office window.

Trenchie was, in turn, the centre of someone else's world. Janine from the police payroll department had her heart set on him. He hadn't noticed. They had been out for lunch on two occasions and she always made a beeline for him whenever they were in the same room. She was very pretty, "flowery" his mum would have called her.

He did like her and enjoyed her company. She would never be Rocco though.

Chapter

9

Glynis very quickly got used to being in the children's home. The first evening in the kitchen area, she got herself a drink of lemon squash and sat down at the table with Layla. The older girl smiled at her gently acknowledging her recent escape.

'So come on, what is it with you, word is, they found you in a graveyard, what do you like about those places then, they give me the creeps, all them dead people?' asked Layla, shuddering at the thought of it.

'I don't know, I just like being there you know, it's quiet and that. I feel safer there than anywhere else.' answered Glynis.

Layla couldn't believe that her new friend had actually spoken. She didn't make anything of it as they talked quietly into the night. Layla told her about her parents, how she was a mixture of Swedish and Australian parents. Her dad had been an Eric Clapton fan and that's why she had the ridiculous name, after some stupid song.

She told Glynis how her mum wanted her to go to Australia because she had a new house there. She had never been there but kept in touch with her mother and wanted to go there one day when she felt ready.

Layla and Glynis had started to form a strong bond. Only because she had studied her new friend over time. So far, it was only because Layla had been consistent, that she had started to trust her. Glynis would talk to her when they were alone, but still not with anyone else.

Everything had been new to Glynis and as time passed, living in the children's care home, Layla had really helped her with her self-confidence and her appearance.

After much determination, Glynis had finally given in to Layla's nagging about letting her braid her hair. She had called them box braids. It took ages to do but Glynis loved her new grown up look. She had no idea she could look so cool.

Chapter 10

Glynis had started to enjoy school, Layla was an A grade student and loved being in class. They helped each other their homework. Layla was a mixture of feisty and friendly. What you saw was what you got with her. Both girls were happy most of the time and made the staff at Heartsholme laugh out loud with their cheeky charm. They could be rowdy and oftentimes they would get up to no good, having second and third helpings of food without asking everyone else. Belching competitions after drinking copious amounts of fizzy pop but overall, they were good kids.

A few lads had started hanging around just along from their school. Johnno was one such lad and he had his heart set on Glynis from the moment he saw her. He was funny and made her laugh, he had olive coloured skin, slightly lighter than hers and she liked that. She didn't speak to him much but she sat on the wall with him after school sometimes, while she waited for Layla to finish her guitar lessons.

Johnno asked her to go out with him but she wasn't allowed boyfriends or dates. It was all in a protection strategy, designed to keep her safe. It was a strict wraparound safeguarding care plan that was adhered to by all of the health professionals involved in her care. Rocco often accompanied Janette to carry out the Safe and Well checks on Glynis. They could turn up at any time without any notice. These were solely in place to make doubly sure that she was safe and to check for any indications that she may have suffered harm either at school or at the children's home.

Because Glynis ran away often, it wasn't practical for Rocco to accompany Janette every time she disappeared but the staff kept a close eye on her with direct contact to both social services and Rocco should anything seem untoward. She always came back before dark and always with Layla. The Children's home really was their home, they loved being there, having their privacy, their own rooms with their personal belongings. Glynis certainly never had anything like it at home. There was a launderette at the children's home, where one of the staff taught them how to separate coloured from white washes, iron and look after their clothes. They learned about personal hygiene, cleanliness and self-respect. Glynis loved it, her independence was growing.

One Tuesday afternoon Johnno waited for Glynis where he knew that she would be hanging around waiting for her friend. He was drinking from a small bottle of vodka and offered her a fresh can of fizzy orange drink.

‘Here, you want some of this in there?’ he gestured the glass bottle towards her can.

Glynis shook her head and quietly said,

‘I don’t think I’ll like it.’

‘Just a little bit, go on, you pour it in, mix it up and see if you like it or not’.

‘Okay then.’ giggled Glynis.

The immediate flavour tasted odd to her, nothing like Glynis had ever tasted before. She had always hated the taste of her mother’s whiskey when she was forced to drink it. She thought that was vile. This was different once it went down though, it was okay.

‘You want a bit more then beautiful?’ asked Johnno.

‘Okay.’ answered Glynis, embarrassed as her cheeks reddened.

Glynis put a bit more vodka in the can, shook it round and then drank it straight down. She smiled at Johnno and they both laughed. It was like a cord had been struck, a line had been crossed. A new experience for her.

Layla came out and she looked tired. She glared at Johnno when she saw that Glynis wasn’t herself, as if he had taken something from her.

‘It’s okay, it’s okay, take a chill pill. I just gave her a small bit of vodka to see if she liked it, and she did, you want some?’

Handing Layla a can of drink he gave her some vodka to put in it. She drank half the can down and added more vodka. They were all laughing and messing about as they walked along the road to the little row of shops. Johnno high fived his friend Fitz and introduced him to Layla. They moved along to the park and swung high on the swings. Fitz showed off his fly offs from swinging so hard and fast and then jumping off at the highest point.

Layla liked Fitz, he was funny and she believed that he cared about her. He always said she was beautiful, how much he loved her long blonde hair. He told her that he wanted to be her boyfriend. The four of them hung out together, whenever and wherever possible, after school for an hour or two, at weekends and holidays. Glynis and Layla were still as close as ever, always looking out for each other.

Neither had ever had sex before and now they were finding out what all that was about. There was a small hut in the park. Like an old bus shelter. They spent a lot of time behind it, taking it in turns to get some privacy, but neither would give in to the boys for full sex.

If they could get out of school, Johnno would take them to the shopping centre, not far out of town and give them money for new clothes and trainers. They both felt like spoilt princesses and continually talked about one day getting married and having the house next door to each other. Being famous and rich like footballers wives.

The more they gave in to, the more money Johnno and Fitz would give them. They got used to it. They loved being outside, being free. Glynis had to ensure a balance between being free and being monitored. She got used to lying to Janette and to Rocco if needed.

'Let's go to my place, come on Glyn you have to do it sometime?' asked Johnno.

'I will if Layla will?' replied Glynis.

Layla agreed to have sex with Fitz and they went back to a flat above a launderette. Johnno said it belonged to his parents. He told them that a cleaner was sent in weekly to keep it spotless, as his parents knew what he was like. They lived mostly in his mother's native country, Qatar.

The flat was clean and tidy and looked quite palatial. Glynis had never seen a bathroom lined with black and gold tiles, she thought it was beautiful. The two double bedrooms were tidy and the beds all well-made and clean, they had bathrooms attached which Layla told her were called en suite.

Sex definitely wasn't what it was cracked up to be. Glynis had always been told that there would be music and candles and that she would feel loved all night long. It was over quickly and she didn't like it at all, it was painful and the noises Johnno made, reminded her of her father. After they had found their way into his bedroom, she had known that what they were doing was very wrong but it made her feel grown up. It was the nearest feeling she had felt to being loved since before her mother's drinking became a problem. Glynis didn't ever want to lose that feeling, so much so, that she would have done just about anything for him.

When they all returned to the living room, Johnno put four pizzas in the oven and they went out onto the veranda to have a cigarette and watch the world go by while they cooked. Another new experience for Glynis, smoking wasn't for her. It hurt her throat and made her feel sick. Layla had smoked since she was nine years old and took all the cigarettes that Fitz gave her.

After their sexual encounters the girls left the flat to go home. Neither of the girls told them where they lived. Johnno had given them some money to get a taxi back as he said they had internet work to do.

'How are you doing with all this Glyn?' asked Layla as they travelled back to the children's home.

'I'm okay, it's all happening fast isn't it, I feel like I'm about eighteen, I like the way that vodka makes me feel though. It's like I can forget everything.' smiled Glynis.

'Let's get back and watch a movie together shall we, I'll get some crisps and that at the shop'.

The children's home was quiet except for Judy on the reception, she gave them a smile as they arrived and asked how they both were.

'Just been to the library.' offered Layla. Judy raised one suspicious eyebrow, leaving them to it.

Back in Layla's room, they got comfortable on her bed and chatted about what had just happened.

'What's that?' said Layla as Glynis pulled out a mobile phone that was beeping incessantly.

'Johnno got it for me, he said it was best that I have one in case he couldn't find me.' answered Glynis.

'What does he want?' asked Layla.

Glynis read the message that said. "Hey Baby Girl, can you meet me tomorrow after school and ask Layla to come, Fitz has got a phone now for her too. Thanks for doing that with me today. I was so stressed out and you made me feel so much better baby".

'We need to be careful Glynis, I promised to look after you. What if one of us gets pregnant?' said Layla.

'He used a Johnnie, ha ha, Johnno used a Johnnie!' cackled Glynis.

They both fell about with the giggles and laughed while they watched a movie on the television.

Glynis texted Johnno back.

'Why were you stressed out though?'

Beeep beeep beep. He replied almost instantaneously.

"Oh you know how it is, I'm in a bit of debt, in a lot of trouble and owe money to some drug dealers. If I don't get it to these guys they have threatened to kill me. I honestly don't know what I'm going to do Baby Girl".

Worried now, Glynis replied quickly.

'I can't help with that can I, I haven't got any money?'

“You could help if you were just nice to the men, just for one evening. They would wipe the debts clean and then we could just be together, but I know you are too young and wouldn’t be able to do that for me. That’s okay Baby Girl, I would understand if you said no”.

Glynis showed the messages to Layla and they were both silent for a while.

‘We do have a good time with them don’t we?’ said Layla

‘I don’t know if I would be able to ‘be nice’ to any men though, do you think you would?’ asked Glynis.

‘Do you think it’s sex they want?’ questioned Layla.

‘Let me text him back and ask.’

“What does being nice to the men actually mean Johnno?”

Johnno answered immediately.

“Oh baby, just to be nice to them, you know, get them a drink when they ask for one, give them cuddles and that, that’s all. If you both did it, you would completely clear our debts for both of us and then we would be free”.

Glynis and Layla agreed to think about it and talk to the boys the next day after school.

Chapter

11

The Galaxy office was pretty much empty as the team supported Hesh, with his mother's funeral.

Mags had rallied round, taking Ruth with her, in the two weeks before, making sure that everyone had the customary white attire for the funeral.

Needing extended compassionate leave from work, Hesh had explained that he would need to be with his family in order to perform "abhisegram" otherwise known as holy bath. Rocco had wanted to know what Amrita would be washed in and Hesh had kindly enlightened her with facts about how the body needed to be bathed with a combination of ghee, honey, milk and yoghurt and that those involved would be reciting mantras.

When they arrived at the funeral service which was held at Hesh and Lilian's house, they were expected to view Amrita's body. The service was led by a Hindu priest who chanted and prayed continuously. Rocco led her team with Trenchie. Mags helped with making sure everyone followed the respectful traditions. Watching

Mark untie his boots was not what she had expected when she had specifically asked the team to wear shoes that could be removed before entering the funeral home.

After the funeral service, the Galaxy Team were not expected to attend the cremation. Hesh told them later that being the eldest son, he had been responsible for pushing the button that controlled the flames in the incinerator. It was what had affected him the most, as his family prayed and he circled the body.

Once the cremation was complete, Hesh took the family to Bradford Beck River which he described as a suitable alternative to the Ganges River, where the ashes were scattered and more prayers were offered.

At the wake Rocco had been talking with her ex-lover Trenchie. Laughing flirtatiously, he had asked her to marry him so that he could take her away on a cruise to the Bahamas for their honeymoon.. They both laughed it off but she knew that he was deadly serious. That ship had long since sailed for her, she was on to someone else.

Rocco managed to get a quick catch with Mags as she told her that she had been on her second date, she had missed this nugget of gossip earlier when Mags had brought in a generous amount of chocolate brownies in the familiar red biscuit tin. It had been break time and the whole team had gathered around her desk to find out how her date had shaped up. They all loved Mags. Rocco laughed with her as she heard some of the meatier details about her second date and made Mags promise to keep her updated.

It had been a long day and Rocco was glad to be back at the Mill. Albie was out in the yard with Conrad and Martin as they fired up the barbecue. On spotting Rocco, Martin came in through the French doors and kissed his sister in law on the cheek before hugging her and picking her up as he always did.

Mark who had been staying late at the office gave Rocco a call to tell her that there had been another child rescue alert for Glynis, but this time Layla had gone missing too. He wanted to let her know because she had an interest in this particular child's welfare for some reason. Replacing the barely used landline, Rocco walked back out to the garden to sit with Albie, her very tall, handsome son.

'Hey Mum, you okay?' he asked.

'Yes my darling, I am now, now I'm here with you.' answered Rocco.

'He still fancies you then babe.' asked Martin, shouting across from the barbecue, smiling at her with his *'I know better than you'* face.

'Oh shut up Martin and give me one of those delicious looking burgers.' Rocco answered, smiling back at him.

'It was Mags who asked him to call me actually, it's about a young prolific absconder from a local children's care home. She's a lovely kid, but she barely talks and is always going missing. She has a huge thing about graveyards which in itself is bloody scary, and I'm not sure she is getting the right help.

Honestly, what some of these kids go through really is unbelievable to most of us.'

'Sounds like a bad case Sis, well at least it sounds like she is one that no one would want to mess with anyway.' said Conrad interrupting his sister and Martin.

MISSING:

Glynis Solomon, last seen at Callachen High Street. DCI Rochelle Raven is appealing for information and asks locals in Callachen and surrounding areas to check dash cams and doorbell video footage from *Tuesday* afternoon.

Please contact us on 101 if you saw Glynis or if you have any information.

Chapter

12

Glynis could just about see through the slit in the blindfold that the building was abandoned, a kind of warehouse. There were metal staircases that zig zagged throughout the space, adjoining rooms and connecting offices. Wires hung from empty, broken electrical sockets like dreadlocks and the smell of old concrete and engine oil filled the air. She could hear men laughing before she even got to the room, where Johnno tied and bound her to a framework.

Another car pulled up, it was Fitz with Layla and she started to call out to her friend.

'Shut your mouth and do as you're told.' she heard Fitz say.

Fitz took Layla into a separate room where four of the men, all from Eastern Europe were waiting for her. As they took turns, Layla left her body, observing the brutal chaos from above, her dissociated self had no emotion, rhythm or rhyme. She watched them systematically assault her young body. Staying dissociated for some time, even after the men had left the room. She saw herself curled up in a protective tight ball, an embryonic residue of pain and humiliation.

It wasn't the first time she had found herself leaving her body or watching similar assaults on herself. It was par for the course, being young and homeless, it was endemic in the system. Power pissed males, social workers, doctors, even homeless support workers, exerting their pathetic sexual prowess like animals. She hated them all.

Some two hours later, once back as a whole person, Layla was able to psychologically put the assault to one side. She'd learned that in order to function, she had to shelve the bad stuff and concentrate on the positive things she had in her life. She carefully uncoiled herself. Her clothes were in a pile on the floor where she had been stripped of them earlier.

She wasn't tied up or bound in any way and right now her only thought was Glynis. Her previous mute state had no doubt, been from some terror or other in her life, and she had to stop anything else happening to her. Putting her clothes back on, she swiftly and quietly crept out of the room. She couldn't believe it was all unlocked and open, was it a test, she thought.

She moved slowly and carefully through the building. Noticing lights on in some of the rooms. The smell of cannabis hung heavy in the air, drying out her throat, it was difficult not to cough but she held it in. The source of the drifting odour soon became obvious.

There were the five men who had just assaulted her, plus Johnny and Fitz, all semi-conscious, snoring, grunting and she noticed a fine thread of dribble running out of the side of one of the fat man's mouth. How she would love to smash his podgy face in. She gathered from personal experience in her young life that they had taken something else, something more than smoking a few joints. Judging by the burned silver foil wraps strewn everywhere. They were all tripping out on heroin.

Just inside that door, she noticed a green woven canvas type rucksack. Like a ninja, she carefully lifted it out through the gap in the door and carried on through the corridors, swiftly, to find her friend.

There were girls tied up in many of the rooms, she caught the eye of a small pale ginger haired girl. She had bundles of glorious curly ginger hair and lots of freckles. She couldn't have been more than ten or eleven. Her eyes were wide, she stared straight through Layla, as if she was asleep with her eyes open. In the next room was another young girl, maybe twelve or thirteen, she was also spaced out and staring up at the ceiling, talking to an invisible entity of heaven knows what. Layla didn't want to leave the girls but she had to find Glynis, if they managed to escape, she would get help for the others. She promised herself that as she kept on searching.

From one room, a low light shimmered through the half open door and she could just make out the sound of a gentle sobbing. She was hoping it was her friend, it had to be her. She moved swiftly into the room and saw Glynis, naked and bound to the railings of the bed on which she had been placed on a disgusting mattress.

‘Have they hurt you?’ whispered Layla.

Glynis shook her head.

‘No, they haven’t but they said were coming back and I was to keep quiet.’

‘They must have been saving you for later then, come on quick we've got to get out of here. I’ll untie you, I've seen a back entrance.’ whispered Layla gently encouraging her friend.

Carefully and quietly they crept out along the metallic chequer plated floor of the corridor, neither of them could believe that they weren’t being followed. It was just getting light as Layla found the way out of the back of the warehouse, through a solid metal door, it was unlocked. They reached a gate, it was locked, Layla scanned a part of the fence near one of the metal fence posts. Using the bolted fixings as steps, they climbed the wire netted barrier.

Glynis tried to muffle her own scream as her foot got trapped in the top fence fixing. Layla managed to free it by dislodging the shoe from her foot. The shoe stayed perfectly wedged in the wire fence. There was a cut in Glynis’s foot which was bleeding so much that they wouldn’t get far without it leaving a trail. Finding a sheltered place just on the other side of a hedge, they sat down and Layla wrapped the gaping wound with one of her own socks. Glynis decided it would be better if she had no shoes rather than just one and left the remaining footwear in the hedge.

Taking her hand, Layla lead Glynis further into the city, dodging being seen as much as possible. Layla spotted a big yellow industrial skip. It was about half full, with what looked like old house and garage clearings. She decided that if they could hide in there for a day or two, it might give them time to rest and give Glynis's foot some healing time, before they carried on.

'One thing we've got to do Layla, is tell someone that there are still girls in that place.' whispered Glynis.

Between them, they made a space in the skip and settled down to hide in silence. Much easier for Glynis as she rarely spoke anyway. Layla pointed to the rucksack.

'Maybe there's a phone in here?'

On opening it she was as surprised as the look on her friends face to see that it was full of money. Bundles of shiny, pink and red, fifty pound notes.

'Look Glynis, when we get out of here, we're going to need to find a safe place for this money. I don't think it'll be safe at the shelter there's thousands of pounds here.' said Layla, smiling.

They both giggled for about an hour in disbelief at the amount of money they now had in their possession. Trying so hard to keep quiet, they laughed silently, looking at one another's face making them both laugh even more.

It was a whole twenty four hours before they emerged, having slept on and off, taking it in turns to listen and to keep watch. It had been raining through the night, the damp and darkness clung on as they climbed out of the cold metal side of the battered yellow skip.

Walking the streets for a while they started to find their bearings. Still on the outskirts of Callachen, they must be somewhere near Hedon Forge Hills, Glynis thought to herself. Layla led the way again and they soon found themselves at a bus station waiting for the number 614 bus, taking them nearer to the children's home address just outside Callachen, a place where they knew they would both feel safe.

When the bus stopped in Callachen, Glynis smiled as she looked across at her friend. Knowing exactly where she was now, she took Layla's hand and guided her along one of the leafier avenues that she knew. The back streets of Bradon in Callachen were like the veins in her body, a warm and intrinsic part of her. Out of breath they reached a graveyard. She steered them to an old toilet block in the middle of the memorial centre. A place where she used to go and hide as a child, when her mother got too drunk. When the beatings got too much. She would always find the most solace in the overgrown part of the cemetery. Her favourite grave had been that of a lady called Mary Meredith Powell: beloved wife, mother, grandmother, sister, auntie and friend to many. Dated 1922 - 1991

'You sure no one saw us?' said Layla.

They sat in the old toilet block to shelter from yet more rain.

‘No one ever comes here, it’s too scary for most people, just pervs and weirdo’s like me.’ said Glynis

The rain stopped and they gradually found their way to Glynis’s favourite part of the graveyard. Glynis sat on the grave with her back against the headstone of the late Mrs Powell. Layla hadn’t ever seen nor experienced her friend as being so comfortable, so happy. It was like she had returned home. Seeing Glynis like this both moved and scared Layla. She was used to her weirdness but this, this was bizarre.

As Glynis sat up against the gravestone, she looked at Layla and gently began to sweep and remove the glassy green gravel from the top surface of the grave with one hand. Then she started digging in the space between the flower holder and the headstone with her bare hands. The ground was soft after the rain, which made the digging effortless for Glynis. It wasn’t the first time she had dug up a resting place of the dead. Smiling to herself as she dug, Layla watched her in silence. When the hole was big enough, they took one bundle of notes out, put the whole rucksack into a plastic bag, cautiously tying the top into two very secure knots.

Layla stood up and had a good look around to make sure no one was watching them. Once clear, they put the whole bag into the deep hole, Glynis started to replace the earth, patting it down like a small child, playing in the sand. Then, she laid out piles of the green shiny pieces of gravel, flattening them across from side to side with her open hands, it was easy for her, like a soil and roots jigsaw puzzle. She had been careful to replace the top weeds and roots as close to how they originally looked as possible. When it was finished, no one would have known that the grave had ever been touched.

'I know you like it here mate, but we've got to get out of it, I want to call the police and tell them about the other girls in that warehouse. We might be able to save them but once those arseholes know we've taken their money, they're going to be mighty pissed off, and we've got to find somewhere safe to sleep tonight.' said Layla.

Glynis nodded, they took a last long look at the grave to make sure that it was perfect and remained looking just as scary to normal people. Making their way out onto the avenue, they went to the first corner shop they could find to get food and drinks and to change one of the fifty pound notes for the bus. Glynis greedily ate three whole packets of cheese and onion crisps and a chocolate bar just while they were waiting to pay.

'That's a big note for a young girl.' said the sales assistant arching one eyebrow.

'Birthday money, why, do you want to make something of it?' shrieked Layla.

'Here's your change, none of my business is it, just get out of here.' replied the assistant, suddenly panicked.

They left the shop, both laughing, repeating over and over again; birthday money, money, money, money.

Layla sang from an old Abba song that her mum used to play on a cassette tape in the car.

‘It’s a rich man’s world.’ Layla shrieked with laughter.

Chapter 13

Johnno and Fitz were scared, they were going to be lynched if Lukas didn't get his money and the girls back.

'We've got to find them, did that Layla ever say anything about where she came from or where she might have gone?' asked Johnno.

'She did mention a children's home type of place that she had stayed in. I can't remember what it was called but I think I know where it is.' replied Fitz.

'If they think they're going to get away with thirty thousand quid, they have got another think coming. And I will personally make sure that they're on that boat to Lithuania myself.' said Johnno, full of rage.

'Do you have to drive so fucking slowly, Jesus! Put your foot down will you?' screamed Johnno.

'Alright, alright I just don't want to draw attention to this car. It's not got any insurance or tax remember?'

The car sped up and eventually came to a stop when Johnno pointed out the road that Fitz had mentioned earlier.

‘Look, there, isn’t that the building you were on about? Let’s park up and pay them a visit shall we.’ Johnno sniggered.

‘Hey man, calm down will you. Have some of this first, you’re always more in control of yourself when you’ve had a line.’

Fitz carefully opened a little paper wrap of white powder and poured it onto a square piece of glass that he kept in the glove box. He chopped it quickly and with the speed and efficiency of a commis chef.

He scraped it across the glass into two lines of white powder, like a miniature snow trail. Johnno rolled a twenty pound note, tight enough for him to snort one of the snowy lines up his left nostril. He always felt like it hit his brain instantly, it froze like ice in his head.

Closing his eyes, Johnno laid his head back on the seat while Fitz inhaled his own white line. Fast and furiously, the cocaine took hold as he held his breath to get the best effects.

‘Good stuff this Fitz, well sourced.’ said Johnno.

‘Mm, sure is mate.’ answered Fitz.

‘Right come on, let’s leave the car here and walk to the place?’ said Johnno.

The Avenue on which the Heartsholme Children's home was based, was lined with Acacia trees. Their defiant roots gnarled as they burst through the concrete slabs, specifically placed around them to keep them in. The trees provided good cover for Johnno and Fitz to hide in wait, while they sussed out the location of their prey.

Lukas Baltakis was getting more and more frustrated as he couldn't get hold of either Johnno or Fitz. He was already planning his return from France to sort this mess out.

Johnno's phone beeped incessantly, it was Lukas. He answered it after the third set of beeps.

'The container leaves for Lithuania in twelve days, get those two girls back and my money. Do you understand? I want my fucking money and if either of these things are not returned to me, you are both dead. Do you understand me?' demanded Lukas through what sounded like gritted teeth.

'Yes Lukas, were on to them now, there was a place one of them said about, where they've lived before and we're watching it now. Don't worry we'll get it all back boss.'

'You had better.' replied the terrifying voice.

The phone went silent.

'Well he is a right piece of work and he scares the shit out of me.' said Fitz still fired from the cocaine rush.

Chapter 14

Layla and Glynis had found their way to a nearby transport café along a long back road towards Callachen. They were tired and hungry but they couldn't risk handing out another fifty pound note. The lady who owned the café was kind and offered them some food if they would wash some pots and help clean up.

Both tall, they looked a lot older than their early teens and their help soon became invaluable to a tired Jackie Francis who had been running the café for eighteen years, mostly alone. She had worked relentlessly, as kitchen hands came and went.

The girls found an old trailer out the back of the transport café. It was like a small shipping container that was warm and dry, they decided to stay in there until they could move on and maybe try and get themselves back to Heartsholme.

There in the dark, Layla asked Glynis how she was feeling about everything that had just happened with the boys and the raping by the old men.

'I don't think they did rape me, they touched me a lot but that doesn't matter to me. I just keep wondering Layla, I mean, it's always on my mind. I can't ever shake it off you know, I keep wondering. Why my mum abandoned me, you know, for the drink I mean. She never used to be so mean and cruel when I was younger.' said Glynis.

'Sometimes drink and drugs does that to people Glyn, sometimes us kids just get caught in the crossfire of their parents shitty lives.' answered Layla, with all the wisdom of a much older girl.

'I'll never understand why I wasn't good enough for her, I was really good, you know. I really tried and now I just feel sick and I want my mum, how she used to be. Why do people just keep on hurting each other,' cried Glynis.

'Come here chick, look it's going to be okay. You're going to need to harden up a bit. She, that mother you knew, she isn't ever coming back and you have got to get used to that. You and me are a team, you've got my back and I've definitely got yours.' said Layla with her arms around a shivering Glynis.

'We'll get these drugs properly out of our systems and get out of here, we'll go back to Heartsholme, we've stayed there so much and maybe we can get back into school, they know us there. We can try and get work in the soup kitchenette this time and stay there for a bit longer, you know, keep out of trouble. Once we're back, you'll be able to have therapy and work with that lovely therapy lady there, she's called Jules. She really helped me once, just after my mum left.' continued Layla.

'I think I need some more of that drug that Johnno gave me, I feel really sick and my foot is killing me.' replied Glynis with one hand on her stomach.

'You have got to just get through it, here look, have some of this water, just sip it though. No one will find us once we're at the shelter and we can get on our feet. Find a place of our own. We've got that money stashed and no one will find it there, not with your graveyard skills.' They both laughed and held on to each other as they settled in to sleep.

Chapter

15

The DAF car transporter with its eight transit vans loaded onto both its lower and upper floating deck, pulled into the layby just before Dieppe. It was due to cross to Newhaven in ninety minutes time. Lukas was old friends with the driver, Thomas McClean and had called him previously that week to get a ride across and back into England.

He needed to find the girls who had disrespected him, his whole operation and who had stolen his money.

Thirty thousand pounds was pocket money in the great scheme of things but that wasn't the point, he had been fleeced and he wasn't going to let them get away with it. He could feel the rage pulsating through his veins, his clenched teeth giving way to a shooting pain in his jaw. He'd tried not to get angry, he knew what the consequences would be. What he could do to people was unthinkable and he had killed many before, who had dared to cross him. People really shouldn't piss him off , he thought to himself and the quickest way to stick a red hot poker up his backside was to steal from him.

These girls were going to get what was coming to them. Climbing into the cab of the lorry, he waited.

Only when all this was over, his last job he kept telling himself. He could return to his new home in France and be left alone.

Chapter

16

The light burned their eyes as the container door opened.

'I thought I saw you go in here last night, what on earth are you doing sleeping rough like this, there are barely any blankets even? Anything could happen to you out here, some of these lorry driver sorts are complete weirdos.' said Jackie, with a mixture of concern and authority.

'Sorry Jackie, we don't have anywhere to go. Truth is we are running from some very bad men who hurt us and they think we've stolen their money. We haven't taken anything honestly and that's why we are working for you.' answered Layla.

'Look let's sit down and talk about this.' answered Jackie.

Sitting inside the café they explained that they had been in care and railroaded into being taken to a warehouse where they were both sexually assaulted. They just needed some time to get back to the care home where they would feel safe and protected from further harm. Jackie agreed to give them some time to get a head start and to get away.

After they left, Jackie gave them two hours, before calling the police.

Chapter 17

Back in the office Hesh said he felt more normal at work than at home and his friends rallied round trying to make him laugh about his late mother and her antics.

He was distracted from his grief by following up a lead that the two girls they were looking for, might be at a homeless shelter because there was data to suggest that they had stayed there before. He had managed to get in touch with a Mr Gilmore (Gilly) the new manager of the children's care home and had gleaned a full history of both girls, when they arrived, what they had been doing and what their routine was.

They had just not returned one day and the manager reported that he hadn't seen them since. Gilly explained that he had taken over from Cynthia after she had retired, he was well aware that she knew the girls better than he did.

Listening in to Hesh's call, Stacey Lord answered a call from a lady called Jackie Francis, a Transport Café owner. She told Stacey that she had information about a couple of girls who had been working for her and needed to report what she knew.

‘Do you want a coffee Hesh?’ asked Stacey as she got up to go to the kitchen.

‘Oh yes please, I’ll come and help.’ followed Hesh.

‘From listening in on your conversation and the call I’ve just had, it sounds like these are linked, we need to draw out some kind of time line don’t we. We’ll brief the others, see where it leads.’ said Stacey.

As Stacey knocked and entered Rocco’s room, she saw Mark quickly move across the room away from Rocco, both slightly red faced.

‘Hi Stacey, what’s up?’ asked Rocco, breaking the silence.

Stacey looked at her boss and then at Mark as he waved to leave the office, Stacey was half smiling, with arched eyebrows. The silence was deafening. The body language intense.

‘Well come on then, what is it?’ laughed Rocco.

‘Ma’am, we think we’ve found a link between the children’s home and the organised crime gang. And then I’ve just received a call from a lady who called to say that she knows the two missing girls and their whereabouts from the last week or so.’ replied Stacey, stifling her curiosity about her boss and Mark Walsh.

‘Right then, let’s go and see this lady shall we?’ said Rocco as she got up, collected her bag and jacket and left the office.

‘We’ll take your car Stacey, you can drive okay?’

Chapter 18

The Heartsholme children's home was just as it used to be. Located just behind a food hall in the busier part of Callachen Town. Glynis kept her head down, nodding where necessary. Gilmore Campbell, otherwise known as Gilly, was a huge Scottish man with a bright red beard and tufts of hair, he was the new manager, a kind man.

'Cynthia isn't here anymore but you know the drill don't you, you can stay here for up to six months at most, and then you need to be out of here. We will help you where we can with interviews, therapy, anything you need. Don't break the rules and especially, don't cause any trouble. No drugs or alcohol or bringing people back. You look after us and we will look after you. It's that simple. Any sign of trouble and you're out, no arguments, no negotiation, got it?'

Both girls nodded just grateful to have a place to stay, to be back in familiar surroundings in a place to feel safe and away from those men.

'Will we be able to have our own rooms again Gilly?' asked Layla.

‘Yes of course you will, we get funded for each room, each young person that walks through the door gets what the funding allocates. You’ve both been here before and you know the score, just behave and there will be no issue.’ Gilly replied, as he showed them to two separate rooms.

‘Lovely this is Gilly, there’s lots of new things too.’ said Layla smiling.

‘We don’t use keys anymore, here are your door passes, you’ve got one for the front door and separate one for each of your rooms. Glynis, this room is 12a and Layla, you’re room is 15b, here you go.’ continued Gilly as he handed the small plastic door fobs to each of the girls.

There were lots of young people in the shelter all doing their own thing. A girl with a shaved head sat in the corner, glaring at the girls as they came in. Glynis had clocked her immediately. She wondered if the bald girl looked angry, or sad, maybe she was sad.

Glynis’s room was a mixture of navy blue and bright orange, it had one wardrobe and three drawers. It smelled of disinfectant and lemons, a huge window that looked out onto the street below. A window lock with a key hanging on an extendable piece of wire was attached to the frame. She lay back on her bed. Apart from this place, she remembered how she had never ever had her own proper bedroom, when her mother was nice she would sleep in her room, sometimes in the bed with her and sometimes in her own bed in the corner. But this place, this was something else. So much better than the last time she was there. She didn't ever want to leave it. There were even coordinating curtains which matched the light and lamp shade. It was perfect for her.

The shelter was noisy but she didn't care, she felt safe in her room and she noticed that there was a lock on the door too. She got up, locked it and lay back down to sleep. She felt exhausted and her foot was hurting a lot. She closed her eyes and started to drift off.

Bang, bang, bang, a knock at her door had her up on her feet in seconds.

'Who is it?' she asked.

'It's me, Layla.' a voice answered.

Glynis turned the silver handle to unlock the door and let her friend in.

'How do you like your room then?' asked Layla.

'I really like it, it feels safe. I just wish I had some of my own stuff to put in those drawers and hang in the wardrobe.' she answered, smiling at Layla.

'We could go and get some stuff, we've got plenty of money, but we've got to be careful.'

Layla was such an old head on young shoulders, she was like a mother to Glynis in so many ways. She reminded Glynis of the early days with her mother, she felt properly cared for.

Bang, bang, bang on the door again. The girls looked at each other, both silent.

'Who is it?' asked Layla through the locked door.

'It's Becky.' answered the voice.

Layla opened the door to the girl with the shaved head. She stepped into the room as Layla moved out of her way.

The girl came in and went directly to Glynis,

'I wanted to give you this.' said the girl.

'Thank you but what is it?' asked Glynis.

'Open it.' said the girl.

Glynis unwrapped the little parcel that had been carefully wrapped and tied with curling ribbon. It was a small metal box that contained a pen, a notebook, eraser and a small pack of colouring pencils. It was like treasure to Glynis because she didn't have anything of her own, she couldn't remember a time when anyone had actually given her a present.

'This is lovely, thank you, why have you given this to me, don't you need it?' asked Glynis.

'I just wanted to make you feel welcome somehow.' said the girl.

Layla beckoned the girl to sit and asked her name.

'I'm Becky, I have had cancer but I'm okay now. My mum and dad died and I didn't have anywhere to go when I got out of hospital, so I live here now until they can find me a foster home. Or I might even get adopted.' said the girl smiling.

Glynis had been right, the girl was sad, not angry. And she just wanted to find friends. They both liked her but were a bit defensive and very protective of their own space and friendship. Glynis winced in pain when she tried to stand to say goodbye to Becky. The girl asked her what was wrong with her foot and told her that there was a medical room just down the hall. A nurse called Megan, was always there for three hours a day and would be there, if she need her foot looking at.

Leaving the room, the two girls thanked Becky and went to the medical centre together, before parting for Layla and Glynis to do some shopping.

The shopping centre was heaving with people, families, couples in love, screaming children and lots of groups of young ones like them. They headed straight for the clothes stores and found some sweat tops, jeans and joggers, hair bands, scrunchies, teen bras and knicker sets. They bought packs of socks, towels and toiletries.

At the shoe shop they bought some new trainers each, although Glynis struggled to get hers on with the bandage that Megan, the nurse had just applied.

They got some odd looks from sales assistants and were asked at least five times if they were with an adult. Every time, Layla just said they were spending their birthday money.

As they were leaving the clothes store they both noticed a beanie hat in the 'Sale' basket, like a lightning bolt they had the exact same thought.

They arrived back at the shelter laden with shopping bags. Taking turns to help each other put the items away they laughed and ate endless crisps and chocolate, washed down with lashings of coca cola. Glynis loved the way the drawers slid open and closed, she became obsessed with them, opening and closing them on their silent runners. Layla laughed at her friend with endearment.

'Come on, let's do my room now.' said Layla.

Stopping on the way at Becky's door, they gave her a knock. She came out tentatively, opening the door just a tiny bit so that she could see who it was. She smiled when she saw the two girls.

'Hey, we bought you something while we were out, got to go now.' said Layla smiling, as they skipped away.

Back in her room, Becky opened the plastic shopping bag which contained a colourful beanie hat and a huge bar of chocolate. Laying back on her bed she held the gifts to her chest. She was so happy, truly happy that someone had thought about her enough to buy her gifts.

Putting the hat on, it fitted perfectly. Taking the wrapper off, she ran her thumb fingernail down the groove of the chocolate foil, removing the silver wrap and broke it in half. She ate the brown sugary treat square by square, slowly, enjoying every moment.

Pouring the carefully prepared mixture of tablets and whiskey down the sink, Becky thought to herself, maybe today wouldn't be the day that she took her own life after all.

Chapter 19

'Hello Mrs Francis, I am DCI Rochelle Raven and this is my colleague Sergeant Stacey Lord.' said Rocco, holding out her warrant card for Jackie Francis to inspect.

'We've come about the girls you rang in about Mrs Francis, what can you tell us?' asked Stacey.

'Hi, Yes come in. It's not Mrs actually but that's okay, just call me Jackie. The girls. Yes, they came in here about a week ago asking for work,. Great little workers, I had no idea they were so young though, they looked much older.

Anyway I gave them some cleaning jobs you know, washing pots and the like. But yesterday I found them sleeping rough in an old container out in the back field. They told me they were being chased by some bad men who had hurt them and for stealing money, which they emphatically denied. Made sense to me though, because why would they be working in a greasy kitchen if they had any money, I know I wouldn't be.' said Jackie Francis

‘What happened when you found them in the container? ‘asked Rocco.

‘Well, I told them they could run or I could help them find help and somewhere decent to live at least. They chose to run and I gave them some time before I called you. Thank goodness because the next day two black BMW cars pulled up and eight of the scariest looking men I’ve ever seen, got out and came in for breakfast. The bloke who I think was the boss, asked me if I had seen two girls and that they had reason to believe they were here.

I thought maybe, one of the other drivers may have seen them and that’s how they had found out they were here. They all bloody stick together that lot, bringing all sorts into this country. I see it all you know.’ said Jackie.

‘Can you describe the men please Jackie?’

‘Foreign, eastern European, Lithuanian I would say, we get a lot in here, truckers, you know, from all over.’

Back in the car Rocco told Stacey that they were on to something bigger than just two runaway girls from a children’s home.

Chapter 20

Ruth had been painstakingly trawling through pages and pages of Lithuanian criminality on the internet, the organisations and associated members of each of the crime cells she had found.

She was surprised to find the amount of young men in the UK who were hugely involved, whilst running somewhat normal lives at the same time. They had been caught previously for trivial crimes involving burner phones or drug dealing in schools and that kind of thing.

Within hours she had enough information on Lukas Baltakis and his army of little helpers to put him away for some time. He was wanted by two separate forces for child trafficking, he had skipped bail from a serious case in Leicester where he had procured groups of teenage boys for a container bound for Delhi.

Nate Bridges was Ruth's Inspector and she looked up to him. Passing the details she had just uncovered to him, he invited her to sit at the briefing table so that they could work through a time line of the events to date with this Lukas, they now had a profile of this person of interest.

She loved his relentless passion for the job, he never left a stone unturned.

He was methodical and she knew she had a great deal to learn from him. They respected each other and their individual strengths.

Laying out the information on pieces of paper initially, the two of them set about speculating how these children could be being so easily manipulated and groomed and exactly how they were getting away with it.

Hesh popped his head in the briefing room door. Nate gestured him in and he asked what they were doing.

As Nate explained, Hesh held his hand up and said,

'Hang on you two I've got more that might interest you, I'll just go and get it.'

Stacey returned with her notes and information from the phone call she'd had with Jackie Francis and the information that Hesh had gleaned earlier from the children home.

'Brilliant mate, this is like one of those big table jigsaw puzzles that my Nan used to have.' said Ruth.

Piecing together everything they had so far, Nate called Mark in to work with them and to bring what he had found.

When Stacey and Rocco arrived back, Mags gestured her head towards the briefing room. They both went in and as they did, everyone looked up.

'What's happening in here then?' asked Rocco.

'We're just putting together a time line of all of our individual information ready to go on the board at tomorrow's briefing Ma'am.' answered Nate.

'That's good, can we have a look now and maybe add some more information. We've just come from a meeting with Jackie Francis, oh I see you already have her on here.'

'Yes, but what did she tell you?' asked Ruth.

'Apparently, the girls have been helping her out in the café for food and staying in an empty container just out the back in a yard, behind her café. She found them and made them tell her what was going on. They told her they had been sexually assaulted in a warehouse by some foreign men, they managed to escape but were being chased because they were accused of stealing money.'

Ruth was writing all of the information down busily on separate pieces of paper, as Nate hesitantly placed them on various spaces of the time line as he continually listened.

'Did they steal the money then Ma'am?' asked Hesh.

‘Well Ms Francis says they didn’t appear to have any money on them and that was why they were working for their food.’ replied Rocco.

‘Where did they go after that, do we know?’ asked Mark.

‘Look guys, let’s get this up on an evidence board. I know you’ve worked hard at this, so let’s get it up to eye level. It might help?’ said Rocco authoritatively.

Without question, George who had since entered the room, pulled a fresh evidence board to the side of the table and offered to pin up the evidence as it unfolded. Rocco used a marker to join up any thinking patterns that had emerged between them.

‘So, from the evidence so far. It looks like we’ve got a worn out old gangster called Lukas Baltakis who is procuring young girls for marketing in other countries. He uses young men and women to do this by encouraging them to befriend the young girls to form so called relationships and then they coerce them into being sexually assaulted by groups of men before being sent abroad?’

Rocco marked the points at which they thought they had evidence to back this up.

Mags brought in trays of refreshments as they worked determinedly, trying to make sense of what they had gleaned so far.

‘Look, we’ll leave it here for today, we all need to sleep on this. Any thoughts anyone, bring them to the briefing in the morning. We can go over this again when we are fresh at it. Thanks guys for starting this. In addition to the existing board, it will really help us in finding these kids.

Chapter 21

George Black was on to something, else. Ruth thought he was useless but finding information on the internet was as easy for him as it was for her. There was a silent clash going on between them that was tangible. It was a sort of competitive, love/hate relationship.

He parked his recent findings as he had been asked by Nate Bridges, to sit in on a video interview with a young girl because he had completed the ABE (achieving best evidence) training in the use of recording equipment. It was second nature to him. He had been recording people since he was a young boy. When he joined the Galaxy Team, George's mother had said

"At least now, he might put his skills to good use instead of following me around like a psycho with a camera."

Ruth wanted to do the training but it was considered an unnecessary expense to have two members of the team trained in the same process, when her expertise could be put to a different use, such as the surveillance of certain persons of interest.

Part of the recording role was in the detailed planning: It was essential to the efficient conduct of any interview with a child. He knew that any strategy agreed, needed to reflect the skills and experience represented by the joint investigating team. A child's interview plan MUST be completed in all cases.

The child had been reported as missing, an anonymous call had come in reporting girls being kept in an old warehouse. Two days later, a second report had come in with her turning up at her home, covered in bruises and having been drugged. After a short stay in hospital coupled with a Forensic Medical Examination (FME), the girl was ready to make a statement.

He had worked out the considerations of the needs of the child, her development and made sure he had the collaboration of the right interviewing officer/s for using appropriate, child friendly language. He knew that Nate and usually Stacey Lord, as interviewers would be aware to explore the child’s social and sexual understanding, her concept of time and who she felt could be trusted and why.

Although he took great pride in the planning, he was more in charge and totally responsible for the provision of video tapes, DVD's and digital recordings stored on video camera hard disc drives. He was the operator. It was his job to ensure that the recording equipment being used was of the highest quality at all times.

George was so clued up that he knew how long to keep the master tapes and anything appertaining to the crime file. He had two cameras which he had affectionately named Stick and Swivel. One of them had to be static and the other had a zoom, pan and tilt facility. The main recording was obtained from the moving camera, whilst the still camera provided a small security picture (picture in picture) in one corner of the screen.

Acting as the operator for these interviews was his absolute favourite part of his job, he always made sure he was available. He knew the cameras would be checked by the interviewer (mostly one of the Galaxy Team) and that any children being interviewed would also be permitted to see and to gain an understanding of how the cameras worked.

When thcy interviewed little Lisa Farrell, the recording started as soon as all involved were in the room.

George Black, Nate Bridges, Stacey Lord, Jillian Mallow, the girls allocated Social Worker and Lisa Farrell identified themselves by name. Once an interview has begun it is best practice that no-one should enter the interview room. Where this cannot be avoided an explanation should be given.

George explained to those involved that the cameras would stay on for the duration of not only the interview but also during any breaks. He explained that it was best practice for either the child or the interviewer, where possible, remain in the room to protect the transparency and integrity of the interview.

It was George's responsibility to monitor the start time of their interview and to ensure there were no issues with the recording. He felt good, he felt like 'somebody special' when he took on this role.

As they got ready to begin, Nate cautiously remembered his own training, he was always nervous around children and had Stacey Lord to sit in. He was acutely aware that one of the key aims of recording early investigative interviews, was to reduce the number of times a child is asked to tell his or her account. His long serving experience told him that even with his skill and judgement, it wasn't an easy task. He knew that this girl might provide less information than she was capable of divulging. He held all hopes on her though, she could be the breakthrough they needed.

Lisa Farrell sat indignantly at having to answer questions that she really didn't want to. At thirteen, she was so clued up about the world. The streets from which she came were full of vodka pickled faces and track suit bottoms. All trying to be better than the others. It was dog eat dog out there, and to be street wise, really was these kids only superpower. She wiped her beautiful red hair from her eyes as she answered Nates first question, asking her where it all started, what had happened?

'I was just hanging out and chatting with my friends at the burger van and then they went home.

Then this bloke came up to me and asked me if I wanted to go to a party, he said all the cool kids would be there.'

'And what happened next?' asked Nate.

'Well I went with them didn't I?' answered Lisa, with attitude.

'What happened next?' continued Nate.

'They took me to a big warehouse place, it was cold, they said the party was in full swing inside, but I suddenly got scared and tried to run. There was a huge wire fence and the gates were locked. This big foreign bloke grabbed me around the waist and carried me back into the warehouse, like a log under his arm. Inside there were eight or nine men.' said a crying Lisa.

'Keep going if you feel okay to.' said Nate, gently.

'I was taken to a room on a filthy mattress, there were other girls, I could hear them crying and screaming out. Those blokes were beating and slapping them, laughing and having their way. I got injected with something and remember seeing and feeling a man on top of me and then I think, no, I'm sure, there was another man waiting to do the same to me. I was so scared, but after that I must have blacked out because the next thing I remember, was seeing a girl looking at me through the door. She said she would get help for us.' answered Lisa.

'Okay then what happened?' asked Nate.

'Are you actually getting off on this or what?' replied Lisa, crying now.

'Lisa, I understand how hard this must be for you, how embarrassing it might be to be telling me, a man about what happened.

I can assure you that I have been helping young girls like you to do interviews like this for a very long time. I really am on your side Lisa. Nothing you tell me will make me think that any of this was your fault okay. If we are going to catch the men who did this to you and to the other girls, we need as much information as we can get, is that okay?'

Lisa cried profusely, Nate was silent for a few moments to let her get the emotion out, gently handing her some tissues and a fresh bottle of water.

'I'm sorry, I'm embarrassed that I got caught up in it and I'm not really sure what they did to me because they drugged me and I don't know anything else, I want to go home now.' said Lisa

'Okay well look, we've got what we need for now, let's give you some space and time to try and feel a bit better. I have arranged for a support worker from the rape crisis centre to come and see you at home tomorrow, is that going to be okay?' said Nate.

Jillian Mallow gently took Lisa's hand and said it would all be okay. She promised to be in on the session with the rape crisis worker the next day if that's what Lisa wanted and they left the interview.

George selected one of the three disks as a master copy, completed the master seal and affixed it to the selected disk. The second and third disk would be used as the working copy and Copy A and identified as such on the disk.

The label had to be fully authorised before the master disk was sealed.

Nate took the disks to ensure that they were kept securely. If what this girl had told them was true, they would soon be rounding up an organised crime gang that had been in operation for some time, pretty much untouched.

Chapter 22

The knock on the thick glass of Rocco's office made her jump again. They were always doing that, she thought to herself! She looked up to see Mark and Hesh, gesturing them in with a smile.

'Ma'am, we've hit on a lead for where the girls might have gone. But we'll need to send in an undercover officer with a body worn camera to see what's going on. I think they might be being targeted as part of that OCG we have uncovered. It looks like they were in preparation to be trafficked as a consignment to be sent to eastern Europe.' explained Mark.

He passed her a file, his hand gently touching hers as he did. It contained the names of some of the gang with the details of Lukas Baltakis as the known leader. She said they looked like thugs in suits.

'Who are you thinking of sending in Mark?' asked Rocco.

'I'll go ma'am, it's just what I need at the moment, an exciting distraction.

I can go full on homeless and I've got my Inspectors Level now, we covered undercover surveillance as well as the UCF (undercover foundation officer) accredited status, so I know exactly what I'm doing.' answered Hesh eagerly.

'Hesh, are you for real? You're far too vain and well-groomed to be homeless looking.' laughed Rocco.

Mark loved to see her laugh and couldn't help himself from laughing with her, almost touching her arm again as he did.

The sexual tension between them was palpable and it made Hesh feel slightly uncomfortable. He couldn't wait to discreetly tell the others. The whole office knew and loved talking about every snippet of information on them.

'I've got my UCF certification on order and it's the only way we can get the information we need. If I can form a relationship with this Johnno and Hesh can get into the homeless shelter, it won't be long before we've got the whole story.' added Mark.

'Right you two, let's just get the basics down, before you both get carried away. I will read the following for you: Firstly, these are both short term operational deployments, because I need you both back here as soon as possible. Secondly, you are to enter into these placements with concealed body worn cameras wherever possible. I want processes, procedures and your accountabilities followed to the letter. Key focus here is to maintain and establish relationships in the two separate scenarios, in order to obtain and to covertly provide us as the Galaxy Team, inside information as a consequence of such a relationship. Is that clear?' commanded Rocco gently but firmly.

'Yes ma'am very clear.' answered Hesh.

'Yes of course ma'am.' followed Mark.

In just a few days with authority granted for the undercover and surveillance operations. Hesh was tasked to go and fit in at the children's home because he looked much younger out of the two. Marks job was to follow and get involved if possible, with one of the two nominals responsible for the two girls being groomed and assaulted.

Hesh was helped by Stacey and Mags to be the best looking homeless person he could be. Mags had been to the local charity shop to find the most fitting clothes and old trainers. She had even managed to find some false tattoos. They succeeded in making his hands look filthy by getting him to plant up some cuttings ready for new pot plants for the office, using soil from the outside break out area.

Hesh was usually very handsome and now looking scruffy and unkempt, he quite liked the mask it gave him. He had always harboured a guilty pleasured yearning, to do amateur dramatics. This was going to be brilliant for him. None of them had ever seen him so excited.

His undercover name was Rab Patel. Stacey dropped him off at the bus station.

'See you later, Rab Baby!' said Stacey as he got out of the car.

Once he was in the shelter he found his way to the soup counter, where he noticed Layla straight away.

He recognised her from the missing persons image in the briefing room. She was serving food in the soup

kitchenette. He made sure the camera was in full view of her as he queued up for his soup.

There was no sign of Glynis. (she was ill in her room, shaking and experiencing cold turkey symptoms from the drugs she had been given by Johnno and the men at the warehouse).

Hesh got talking to Layla quite quickly, she came and sat with him in her break to eat her own soup. She was very closed, answering only yes or no to him, which made them both laugh.

'What is this, trust nobody thing, you've got going on then?' said Hesh.

'Well you're right Rab, I don't trust anyone at all, well except my mate Glynis, I trust her with my life.'

Just at that moment Glynis arrived and joined them at the table. Hesh had never seen such beautiful eyes in anyone and couldn't take his eyes off of her. He wondered if she was wearing contact lenses.

'Stop staring at her Rab.' said Layla, stifling a laugh..

‘Sorry, sorry, I was just mesmerised by your eyes Glynis they’re a very unusual colour aren’t they, they seem to change from amber to brown, depending on the light?’

Glynis didn’t reply, she just looked at him and then smiled at her friend.

‘You must be feeling better then mate, go and get some soup Glynis, it’s really good today and there’s some gorgeous bread to go with it’ smiled Layla.

Glynis said nothing as she got up to go to the counter. Hesh kept his cool and started rolling a cigarette.

‘She’s a cool one?’ he said.

‘She’s alright, just doesn’t like to talk much. Well, she does to me but that’s okay, she trusts me. What brought you here anyway, what’s your story?’ answered Layla.

Drawing from a recent case that the team had worked on, Hesh recalled it as if it was his own life.

‘Well my dad died and then my Mum remarried a bloke called Jason. He hated me and made my life hell, he was into little boys, if you know what I mean. I had to get the hell out of there, I couldn’t bear to be in the same room as him. So I left. I’ve been on the streets for a few years and then I ended up here because they give food out to the homeless. If there’s a room available in the old part of the building, Gilly sometimes lets me kip here too.’ replied Hesh, eyes watering.

Just as he finished talking, Glynis came back to the table and started eating her soup.

She said nothing. Layla got up to get back to the soup counter and Hesh asked if it was okay if he stayed sat where he was.

Glynis nodded at him.

‘Look, I know talking isn’t your thing. I’ll just talk about me.’ smiled Hesh.

He told her a long worn out story of his time as a child, when his family were happy, when he and his parents and three other siblings went to Pakistan for the first time. Before the shit kicked in with his evil step father, Jason.

Glynis listened intently, watching his every move, and taking in his body language. Something wasn’t quite right about him but she couldn’t quite work out what it was.

Chapter

23

Jules's counselling room was not like any of the psychology places Glynis had ever been, like at the doctors or the hospital. It wasn't clinical at all.

The first thing Jules asked Glynis was whether or not she would like a drink. She settled for squash and they sat down to talk.

After the general terms and conditions were established and Glynis fully understood the confidentiality clauses. Jules wrote a life/time line in chronological years on a piece of paper, from Glynis's birth to the current date. They explored the experiences that Glynis considered to be the worst traumatic experiences and how she had coped throughout them. On each one, she was asked to consider whether her feelings about the incident were high or low. She was asked to score on a scale of one to ten. One being the lowest distress level that she could possibly feel.

For the first time in her young life, Glynis didn't stop talking. She had never spoken so much to anyone.

Jules reminded her of her mother, the mother that she remembered, before she had become a drunken monster.

Jules suggested doing a session of guided visualisation so that they could go back and revisit her childhood memories. She explained that it might be very emotional for her. How it was a very powerful tool which would help her to go back, to revisit, and to make changes in her previous situations. Jules explained how this would help her to create a calmness that she wasn't able to do anything about at the time.

She explained that it was useful to have some music in the background and if she felt okay with that. She also offered her a rather large comfy blanket, to avoid her feeling too exposed, as she recalled any childhood memories that came up for her.

Glynis agreed to thc process and tentatively laid down on the couch to get relaxed, whilst Jules put on some soft, soothing music.

Jules began by reading out the initial guidelines;

'Guided Visualisation allows the choice of time and space in the safety of one's own environment where disturbance can be minimal and relaxation can be attained, in order to feel the letting go of many painful memories.'

Jules asked Glynis to relax and to just lie back, she gently and gradually talked to her, went through each muscle group, tightening and relaxing to help her to feel safe and calm.

'All you need to do right now Glynis, is relax and let the sounds drift over you, get yourself comfortable with as loosely fitting clothing as possible and just relax, you have given yourself this time for you to just be...so that's it now...just be...

Making yourself comfortable will give you all the right reasons to pay attention to your breathing.

When you have finished listening to this guided visualisation here with me today, you will awaken slowly, with a sense of inner calm and freedom.

So now, notice your breathing, the soft in and out that naturally and instinctively happens all by itself. And, as you relax, take some deeper breaths. Gently breathing in and gently breathing out, all is safe and all is calm.'

Jules asked her to go deeper and deeper until she was at the bottom of a very beautiful slope, by counting her steps down the slope.

'I will count them for you now so that ....just to help you move along and go further down.

10 Feeling slightly nervous

9 Notice the gradient as the surface slopes down and deeper down

8 Smiling as you get going further down

7 Feeling lighter and more and more relaxed

5 Allowing the relaxation to take over

6 Further down now

4 Going deeper and deeper down

3 Just let it go now as you make your way down the slope

2 Feeling the peace as you go further down

1 And here you are

Now you are at the bottom of a beautiful slope. You are in a complete weightless state of mind, free and safe, getting ready to reflect on your past.

So now, just take yourself somewhere up into your mind and imagine that you are outside in a garden on a warm sunny day, maybe in your childhood. This may be a special place for you or somewhere in your imagination.

Imagine a beautiful summer's day, feel the soft breeze to cool you and hear the sounds of nature all around. Okay Glynis just imagine that you are looking up into the sky.

Remember a happy time in the past when you were relaxed……nothing at all to do……nothing at all to worry about…….feeling really good about yourself……Now while you are here with me relaxed, safe and protected, relaxed and at ease just let your mind float back in time to your early days……as if there is no gap, now is then and then is now.'

Jules had a soothing, warm voice and Glynis had no problem going along with it. It was the most relaxed she had ever felt in her life.

'Go back, back, back to your own childhood. Notice how everything changed so quickly in so many areas of your

life when you were a child.

You were so unaware of good people and bad people. You didn't know the difference. You had to do what you were told and so you did.

Remember when so many things were so new to you Glynis. There were lots of first times and new beginnings. School, that was strange and exciting and sometimes you may have been afraid. Going up to the next level in school, all strange and new and exciting in equal measure. Then all the after school clubs, relationships in school. Your first ever friendship ……all just as strange………just as new……and all the first times and new experiences.'

Jules continued asking her to let her mind go to an age that she could most remember and that when she arrived at that age, to think about where she might go on her own when she was sad, scared or unhappy?

'I went to the garage in the garden and then later, when I was older, I went to the toilet block in the graveyard, it always the toilets, I felt safe there.' whispered Glynis

'Okay, so now we have built up a picture of you and you can just see yourself sitting in yours place thinking about all the things that happened or were happening at that time, feeling all those feelings just as you did then, can you see that?'

As Glynis started to relax, she drifted off into to her childhood. She saw herself on her mother's lap, they were singing. She must have been tiny, maybe twelve months old or just over. Jules watched as tears rolled down her clients face.

The memories continued for Glynis as she related exactly what was going on to Jules.

Suddenly Glynis let out a high pitch scream.

'No, no, no not that! Why did you take her, why, why, why.'

Glynis had learned very quickly to remove herself from her body and from any situation. But now, now she was seeing everything that happened on one day in her childhood as clear as day. She had been told many times that she dissociated and this was possibly why she always felt unable to talk at any level of understanding. Inside she had become rigid with fear.

A previous psychologist had said that the process of dissociation could be simplified, to equate to creatively shutting off in childhood. In order to not see the reality, to enable survival of the traumatic events which present in that 'here and now' experience for a child.

What Glynis was seeing made so much sense to her, the garden of her childhood house, the garage that her father built and her incessant need to be in that garden whenever possible. She couldn't quite make the connection but this was around the time that her mother started drinking, that she changed towards Glynis, beyond all measure.

'Okay Glynis, you're doing really really well. Now, I want you to be in that place, with the younger you. Be the older version of you, that you are today, the Glynis who is in this room.

Walk over to the younger you, that you were then and sit down at the side of her. Put your arm around her, hold her tight, and tell her everything she wanted to know and feel free to do that aloud or in your own head.
Be sure to tell her that everything is going to be alright. You know more than I do, exactly what she wanted and needed to hear then, so tell her.

That's it, keep holding her in your arms, and as you do, keep loving her, even holding on to her so tightly that you can imagine pulling her back inside where she belongs and you can take her down to a warm safe place deep inside you.

A place where she will be safe and protected and you can allow her now to sleep peacefully within you as the young adult you are today. Because she's been outside for a long time. And it's now time for you to take care of her and allow the real you to evolve and to grow up in the way she wants to.

Because Glynis, I know that you want to take good care of her and from this day forward you can just let go and not allow anyone or anything to hold you back from having a full and happy life.

It's your turn now to be happy with your life in the way you choose to live it, for yourself and to enjoy every moment. Because you know……your life can be whatever you want it to be and these new feelings of inner happiness and complete freedom and of knowing that your new future into adulthood is going to be full of love and fresh opportunities.'

Glynis continued to cry silently at the recalled event that she had just witnessed and the tears soaked her face, trickling down into the tiny crevices in her young neck. She didn't notice.

Jules talked her back up and out of the visualisation.

'Okay, so now I'm going to help you walk back up that slope to a new awareness and a new beginning. I will count you back up, just as I did going down. So listen for my cue as I start now:

1 You're now going to begin the journey back to this room.

2 Start to move slowly.

3 Feel the new you, starting to grow into a young adult.

4 Up and up the slope – feeling energized as you move.

5 Leaving all those bad memories in this room with me.

6 Focusing on positive and new beginnings.

7 Up and up you come.

8 Feeling refreshed and alive.

9 Feeling confident and relaxed.

10 Returning to normal wakeful awareness.

That's it Glynis now sit up slowly and have a breather and a drink'. said Jules, calmly.

'That was weird and I feel a bit sick to be honest'. answered Glynis.

'Here, drink a little water. Are you able to tell me what happened in there, it sounded like you remembered something terrible?' asked Jules.

'I just can't talk about it, I don't want to remember what happened. But at least now I know why my mother hated me so much.' she answered.

Chapter

24

Ruth McCarthy laughed out loud and fist bumped the air as she finally uncovered the evidence that she had been searching for of a trafficking gang who were laundering money through a chain of small grocery shops. With her vast experience of hacking into group forums, echo chambers and rainbow tables, she had found it quite effortlessly.

Both Mark and Nate were very happy with her internet skills but less impressed with her time keeping and loudness. Mags thought she was hilarious and became entertained by the others obvious disdain of her regular outbursts.

Ruth preferred to keep working and to eat at her desk, she ate loudly and slurped her regular supply of fizzy drinks, usually through a straw, right down to the bottom of the carton very loudly and blissfully unaware of the noxious effect it had on those around her. This often resulted in a huge belching session which would cause the office to empty pretty rapidly.

It was after one of these such lunchtimes that Nate had been following the lead on the Lithuanian nominal, Lukas Baltakis. He was definitely the ringleader of an organised crime gang who had already been marked for trafficking women and/or young children to Lithuania, where he had clients waiting.

On uncovering some of the details it seemed that his next consignment was specifically for very young girls, between ten and thirteen years old.

With the evidence in the statement from the young girl who had recently given a video interview, he had hit a match. It was too much of a coincidence that the young red haired girl had described the gang of eastern European men. How they had drugged and sexually assaulted her and then for them to actually locate a group matching their descriptions.

The grocery shop money laundering that Ruth had come across earlier, was exactly what he was looking for and he requested a copy link to be sent to him.

It was Nates turn to fist bump the air. The grocery shop was on the corner of Drysdale Road, just outside the centre of Callachen high street.

Slipping on his jacket, he decided to pay them a visit. It was easy enough to park as he arrived at the store. Purchasing a big box of assorted chocolates for his Mum and six cans of lager for his brother, he paid with one of the notes he'd been given by his fraud investigation colleagues.

The cashier smiled and handed him his change which consisted of one counterfeit twenty pound note and two counterfeit five pound notes together with some change.

Back in his car he smiled to himself. They had them bang on. They just had to prove it now.

Chapter

25

With his dreadlocks always beautifully kept in pretty much symmetrical braids, Mark found it harder than Hesh to rough himself up. The Galaxy Team had great fun with him, getting him to try on different clothes.

Once again, Mags had acquired some suitable trainers.

Stacey had a niece with dreadlocks and knew how to tease the hairs out just enough for them to look less well-ordered. In the last few days since awaiting the UCF confirmation, he hadn't shaved and it surprised him, just how much facial hair he could produce in such a short space of time.

Mark was going for a kind of, old London, Bill Sykes look. Donning a rastacap to tuck away most of his dreadlocks, he was starting to fit the image he needed. His undercover name was Lebor Shanson, homage to an old school friend.

Following a lead from Nate to the 'Beat Market' grocery shop on the corner of Drysdale Road, he made his way. Taking a few sips of whiskey from a small square flask kept on the inside of his jacket. He lit one of the Marlboro lights he had hung on to from years gone by. If he was going to meet with one the crime gang, he wanted to at least smell the part.

George had wired him up so discreetly that the body worn camera was part of a button on his scruffy old jacket. He laughed as he likened it to a Bond film and thought to himself that Rocco might be his Moneypenny if he was successful at bringing this lot in. Or she might even invite him for dinner some time. He loved to dream.

Arriving at the shop, he went inside, loitering around the counter, waiting for the last two customers to leave.

The man serving looked at him and smiled on one side of his mouth only, as if knowing he wasn't there to buy groceries.

'Alright? I'm looking for some gear man, I'm told you will see me right?' said Mark, visibly shaking for maximum effect.

'It's not here, hold on I need to make a call.' said the shop man.

When he came back out to the front of the shop, he handed Mark a slip paper and said,

'Meet him here in thirty minutes right?'

'Right, thanks man.' replied Mark.

Mark waited at the Bilberstone Park entrance, on a bench, just by the green bin, as instructed.

Within thirty minutes, two young hoods were walking towards him. Discreetly making sure his camera was switched on, he feigned his shaking hands again and started rocking, one foot incessantly moving up and down, up and down. He had seen enough drug users in his time to know how to behave like one.

'Fuck you're well in need man or what?' said Johnno.

'Just give me some gear man, will you?' said Mark, feigning desperation.

'Now let's sit down here with you and have a little chat man, what do you need, I mean really need?' asked Fitz.

'I want some ganja and then I want a dragon chaser, can you do that for me man?' pleaded Mark, eyes wide open.

'Anything else?' said Johnno, eyes raised.

'Well, like what?' answered Mark, accelerating the shaking and anxiety act.

'Girls, you want some baby girls man?' we can do that for you for two hundred an hour, here in the park tonight?'

'Yeah man, that be beaut…i….ful, but I haven't got that kind of money today. I'll have it by Friday when I get me benefits, can you wait?' said Mark pretending to be keen and eager for a young girl. It made him sick to the stomach and he tried to replace the image of a child with one of Rocco, laughing.

It worked, Johnno and Fitz saw the hunger in his eyes and told him they would be back on Friday.

Johnno gave him an eighth of marijuana and a small wrap of heroin. He handed over some dirty notes in exchange and nodded subserviently towards them as if he were a lowly follower of their criminal power.

'Don't take it all at once man, we want to see you here on Friday, make it later on though, about eight, it's better in the dark, know what I mean?' winked Fitz.

Mark nodded again. He was fuming and waited for forty minutes until he knew they must definitely be gone. Slowly, he gathered himself and with the drugs in his pocket, he walked out and away from the park.

He got on a bus and found his way to the arranged meet with Stacey.

'What happened Mark, you don't look too happy mate?' asked Stacey.

'Bastards, they were so cocky! They offered me drugs and young girls, children. It took me everything I had to not smash their putrid little faces in there and then.' growled Mark.

Smiling, Stacey wanted to say how he could have thought about Rocco to help. She decided not to, having no real idea how close to the truth she actually was.

‘Okay well look, we need to continue, what’s the plan for hooking up with them again?’ asked Stacey.

‘I’m meeting them at the park on Friday, about eight o’clock.’

‘I’m going to speak to Rocco and see if she can get authorisation to get some covert cameras set up in the park as well as your button hole. It could be our best evidence to date.’ said Stacey.

‘Yes that’ll be a good move Stace.’ answered Mark.

‘You get home and stay there until Friday, we can’t risk you being seen. You have access to everything from there anyway don’t you?’

‘Yes of course, stay in touch and keep me up to date with everything okay?’ asked Mark.

Chapter

26

Lukas had made it safely back to England. He had been watching the Heartsholme children's home for about eight hours after Johnno and Fitz had given him the details. He and three of his thick ugly henchmen were disguised with black clothing and armed. Like thunder, without any warning, Lukas and two of the men stormed the Heartsholme Children's home, looking for Glynis and Layla. Hesh recognised him instantly from the intel he'd seen on the evidence board and from the intelligence he had been sent by Ruth.

Hesh knew it was going to be bad and searched for Layla and Glynis. Luckily for him and them, they were both in a corridor together, running down to the reception to see what was going on.

He grabbed them both telling them to keep quiet, pulling them into a small cupboard. It had been set up as a safe room and there was no way it could be accessed from the outside. He held them in there, quiet and close. He whispered to them to keep quiet and still. They all heard the shooting and shouting, both girls were terrified that they were going to die. They heard Gilly shout at the men to get out as a shot was fired and he went quiet. A child ran across the reception and she too was shot. Chaos had erupted, people were screaming and shouting. And then suddenly, it was silent.

In the cupboard they waited, frozen as they heard footsteps walk passed the door.

The familiar sound of Eastern European voices made his ears prick up. Hesh was sweating profusely, he managed to get a message to the office, he didn't think his camera would work because of the darkness. He requested full back up and ambulances.

Hesh was good with languages, he always had been. He'd heard the shout.

'jų čia nėra.' which he knew that in Lithuanian, meant something like 'they're not here.'

He decided that it would be safer to just sit tight, to keep quiet. Keep them all safe in silence. Back up was on its way. He was not comfortable with being shut in a cupboard though, he felt sick and his sweating worsened.

His breathing was panicked. Layla could see he was struggling and reached for his hand to comfort him. She whispered for him to breathe through his nose and out of his mouth. He tried to do it quietly and it seemed to help a bit. He nodded briefly and smiled at Layla as if to thank her.

None of them uttered a word. They stayed frozen as silence reigned in the adjoining corridor, until they suddenly heard a cacophony of emergency service sirens.

Trusting it was safe, Hesh carefully unbolted the door and they made their way out of the cupboard. He told them to go back to their rooms and that someone would come and get them.

He crept down to the reception and just as the armed officers were entering and taking over the scene. It was carnage, there were two bodies, one slumped across the reception desk. A child lay bleeding on the ground, it was Becky.

The camera in Hesh's button hole was still running the intel back to the office which was in turn, channelled to other units, including the armed police unit.

An eager cop named John Ronsell tried to arrest Hesh but he held his hands up. I'm police. I'm Job, I'm undercover police. There are two girls we have to keep them safe and get them out of here, they're what this is all about, come with me.

'Stay here, we don't know if there are any gun men still in the building. Just fucking wait here until we're done.' shouted the commanding officer, Max Gaunt.

Hesh refrained from argument as he let the team do their job, he was just glad to be out of that cupboard, to be free and to cool down a bit. His breathing took a while to return to some kind of normality. Head in his hands, he watched the paramedics working on the man and the young girl who he had come to know as a good kid, she was sweet, needy and completely lost in her young life.

It was a miracle that both were still alive and he wondered to himself if either would survive their injuries.

Max Gaunt walked briskly back from the corridor ordering Hesh to go to the girls who were terrified and waiting for help. He obeyed because it was easier. Getting up, he hurried back to their rooms. They were huddled together in Layla's room.

'Rab are you okay. We were so worried that you'd been shot?' said Layla concerned.

'Hey, yes I'm fine, just a little stressed out from being in that cupboard. Now you two, you've got to listen to me okay. I'm a police officer, my real name is Hesh. I work in the Callachen missing children unit and we're investigating a grooming and trafficking gang that we believe you may indirectly be involved with.'

'It doesn't surprise me at all, I knew there was something different about you.' said Glynis quietly.

Both Hesh and Layla were thrown at the fact that Glynis had spoken to anyone except Layla.

'Well, look maybe that's a good thing because otherwise we would be dead by now.' said Layla trying to stay positive.

'I'm going to ask that you both come with us, we will keep you safe, I promise, but you can't stay here. In case they come back for you, okay?' said Hesh

'Are we going to be in trouble?' asked Glynis.

'No, no, not at all. I promise. We will need some information though, if you can help us with what you already know. That's all. Promise.' smiled Hesh.

'Can we take our stuff with us?' asked Glynis.

Both girls told Hesh that they needed to move on. They were allowed to take their belongings and Hesh arranged for Janette the social worker, who was now working for both Layla and Glynis, to find them alternative accommodation.

Janette spoke with Rocco and with authorisation and assistance from Trenchie, the girls were soon relocated to a safe house not too far away. There was some meaning in the seeming madness of hiding in plain sight.

Janette had only agreed to this because she was adamant that Glynis could continue with her therapy as she had learned so much. Her mental health was improving and she had grown so much in self-confidence.

The safe house was with a couple called Melanie and Arnold Malachy. They were ex police officers and had set the house up with expert knowledge. Both girls had separate bedrooms which had their own en suite bathroom. It reminded Glynis of the flat that her and Layla had been to with Johnno and Fitz.

The house was Edwardian and the rooms were huge. It was palatial in fact. Glynis loved it. They both laid out on the huge king size bed in Layla's room and laughed until they cried at everything that they had already endured in their very short lives this far.

It wasn't long before they both fell asleep. They were exhausted from the trauma of the gun incident, fear for their lives and fear of having to give their money back.

Chapter

27

Johnno and Fitz loitered in the park, smoking and drinking from cans of beer. They were laughing, sort of howling and trying to intimidate late passers-by, like a couple of hyena's.

Walking slovenly towards them, a scruffy Mark Walsh aka Lebor Shanson, smiled a half smile.

'You got my gear?' asked Mark quietly, avoiding eye contact, faking his usual hand shaking and stuttering behaviours.

'Yeah, we've got what you need man.' answered Johnno.

'And the girl, you got the girl?' asked Mark, purposefully, licking his lips.

'If you got the money, you meet us over there by that old cricket hut in fifteen minutes, we'll bring her, right?' replied Johnno.

'Yes, I've got the money. I'll go there now.' said Mark.

Mark waited by an old wooden hut that was painted green. The paint had long since peeled off to leave a slight green tinge of residue in its grooves and lines. From a distance it could be argued that it was still fully painted green.

He rolled a cigarette and lit it, drawing on it he pretended to busy himself by looking at an old phone he had.

Through a side glance, he saw Johnno walking up to the hut with a young girl, he could see that she was mixed race like him. He wondered if there had been a reason for that choice and quickly set it aside. She looked frightened.

'Here's the kid, take her. You've got one hour with her, you can do what you want with her just don't leave any marks. Now give me the money.'

Johnno handed the girl to Mark and they exchanged money. Johnno counted out twenty of the new purple, waxy ten pound notes and smiled.

'That'll do nicely sir, best benefit money you'll ever spend that is. I'll be back in an hour.'

Mark took the young girls hand and they walked away towards the toilet block. He knew that Johnno and the other one was watching him so he had to be careful.

'What's your name sweetie?' he asked the young girl.

'Matilda.' she stuttered.

‘Listen to me, I have come to get you away from these men but we have to pretend that I’m one of the nasty ones okay. In about fifteen minutes, this park will be swarming with police. Do you understand what I’m telling you Matilda?’

‘Yes, I think so.’ said the girl, nodding.

True to his word, Johnno and Fitz barely made the gate before they were approached by two intimidating police Belgian Malinois Shepherd dogs, on very long leashes.

‘Put the drugs on the ground and keep still or we’ll let the dogs off.’ shouted the police dog handler.

Both completely froze after emptying their pockets and laying the contents on the ground. Another two officers quickly handcuffed them both and walked them into an awaiting police van.

Mark and Matilda waved as he caught Johnno and Fitz’s glance and walked the girl to another police car, where she was covered with a blanket and taken to the social services offices.

Chapter

28

Hesh returned to the office and headed straight for the shower room after submitting his camera for the footage and completing the paperwork. Mags always helped him enormously with his paperwork, enough so, so that he basically had to just fill in the gaps.

The following day, interviews had been set up for Glynis and Layla separately.

At Glynis's interview she looked all around as the tape recorder made its usual long high pitch sound. Rocco reiterated that she wasn't in any trouble.

Those present gave their names, which were PC Mahesh Patel, DCI Rochelle Raven, Janette Sullivan and Glynis Solomon.

Hesh and Rocco were both kind to her and offered her a kind of promise/ resolution which they thought would solve everyone's problems.

‘We want to keep you safe under the council authority if you agree to help us bring in Lukas and the boys who gave you drugs and hurt you?’

‘How do you know they hurt us?’ asked Glynis, defiantly.

‘Because we have evidence from another girl who was held captive and sexually assaulted at the same warehouse where you told another witness that you were taken.’

Glynis quickly tried to compute who these other people could possibly be.

‘Did the other girl have ginger hair?’ asked Glynis innocently.

‘Yes she does.’ replied Hesh.

Glynis looked to the floor, secretly grateful that it may have been her phone call after they had got out of the skip, that saved the ginger haired girl.

‘We already have intelligence to suggest that they are collecting young girls to traffic. You were lucky to have escaped like you did. So, we will need to know where you were taken, what happened and what you believe is going to happen to you if they find you, if that’s possible?’ said Rocco.

‘Will I still be able to see Jules?’ asked Glynis, quietly.

'Yes, I will make sure of it, although we will need to source a different meeting place for you both, just to keep you safe, okay?' replied Rocco.

'Yes, we can arrange that at the contact centre Glynis, so don't worry about that at all.' chipped in Janette, smiling.

'Okay so I first met Johnno at the school, him and his mate were always there, giving us drinks and that. I thought he was my boyfriend and that he loved me. But now I know he just wanted me to have sex with his friends.' said Glynis.

Rocco gathered information about Johnno and Fitz as she knew they were also waiting to be interviewed.

Glynis told them everything exactly as it happened, as did Layla. But neither mentioned or admitted to any money being stolen.

Chapter 29

At the next therapy session, which had been arranged to take place at a contact centre within a social services building for safety's sake. Jules listened intently to the latest disturbing developments at the Children's home. Glynis told her that they had been moved to a safe house since the incident in case anything else should happen or them getting found by the gang that were after them. Glynis had been warned not to disclose her new address to anyone. Not even to Jules.

Glynis recalled her recent panic attack experiences, they had stopped for a while after she met her friend Layla. But she had been having them since childhood. She told Jules how since the last session where they did the guided visualisation, she could suddenly hear her own heart beating, how she felt unable to breathe.

Jules explained her knowledge of panic attacks.

'Those feelings which are so unfamiliar, they create a feeling in which, you actually believe that you are going to die, you are in fact, abreacting. In other words, the memory is so profound that it feels like you are back at the incident to the point where adrenaline has been released from your adrenal glands (situated just above your kidneys).

For the technical terms and I know how you love inside knowledge Glynis. This means that red blood cells flood to carry oxygen, then, blood is diverted to wherever it is needed. Your breathing becomes rapid to provide you with more energy. Your lungs dilate to give you more oxygen but it's only an abreacted memory.'

'So why do I feel so scared then, if it's protecting me?' asked Glynis.

'Because your body thinks and feels as if it is still there, in that terror moment. It's a bit like what happened the last time you were here, but worse. Your sweating increased and you felt sick, but you can't be. Just like you felt here, remember?'

'Yes I do, I couldn't be sick but I felt like I wanted to be all night and I had the runs too.'

'Yes that's all part of it too. While having a panic attack you will nearly always need the toilet badly. It's perfectly normal Glynis, It's your body's way of making your body lighter for purposes of flight. Your muscles will have tightened and you can become like a coiled spring. Your blood pressure can raise too, as your body reminds you of the previous experience. I promise that it is your body protecting you.' reassured Jules.

‘But it comes on so quickly Jules, I don’t seem to have any control over it and it scares me. It’s like I have no control of myself.’ questioned Glynis.’

‘Yes, I can’t tell you how completely normal this is. These physical responses can happen to you in a split second, even though it might feel and seems much longer. The silence in your head is often deafening as you endure these ruminations and memories, as your brain appears to be hijacked by the terror that you have experienced and by everything else that happened to you.’ continued Jules.

‘I always feel so angry, it’s so painful in my heart, thinking about my Mum and what happened.’ said Glynis, extremely upset.

‘Listen Glynis, I don’t know what it is that you saw when we did the visualisation and maybe one day when you are ready, you will tell me. But you have got to give yourself time to heal, to make as much time for yourself as you can. I know you’ve got school and you probably have to tow the line more tightly than usual in the new safe house. But you’re young and you will get through this. I promise that it will all come together in the end. Listen to this quote about trauma:

“Traumatic incidents, whether they happen in childhood or as adults, whether we witness them or experience them. It is what has happened to us and not what we have created.”

It makes sense doesn't it? It's not about what you did to make any of this happen. It's about what ***happened*** to you?' continued Jules.

'I suppose so and I still have so much anger in me.' answered Glynis.

'Let's look at your anger shall we?'

'Yes, I guess I need to try and understand it.'

'Well, what can I tell you about anger. I can tell you that it's often underpinned by pain and frustration, at what happened. It could be towards those who have hurt you, your friends and family. Possibly added to the mix is that you are unable to talk about it with loved ones, because they aren't available. But I'm here. You can come to me for as long as you need to. Don't worry too much about that old anger. It is often called the backbone of healing, a powerful and freeing force, a superpower in fact.' said Jules, half smiling.

'I need to know what to do with it, sometimes I want to scream and shout and even kill people. My friend Layla helps me a lot. She keeps me calm and I feel safe with her, she gets me to do the breathing thing.' said Glynis.

'Okay well look, there are positive ways to channel this anger, physical activity, you know, get out and do stuff outside. You can talk to someone like Layla or me or a teacher at school. Just someone who you trust. You can write a journal of your experience to alleviate the way you feel and transform those feelings into a healthier emotion.' answered Jules.'

Glynis remembered the notebook that Becky had given her. She thought about how she would start journaling when she got back to her room.

'Glynis, look, I know that you are full of disbelief and shock about what you saw in that visualisation. It's only the beginning and it will be hard to come to terms with what has happened. For a while, life may seem chaotic, you may go over and over scenes in your mind unable to shut it out.

These thoughts might take up a lot of your thinking time. For one so young, that may be difficult because it leaves no space for anything else in your life. I know it can be distressing, disturbing and at times it will affect your mind balance. But I must keep reminding you that it's important to know that this will not last forever and it really is possible to put the pieces of your life back together and to move on, and I will be there for as long as you need me okay?' said Jules.

'Look I need to go back to the safe house and have a lie down I think. I'm feeling really tired.' answered Glynis.

'Yes, you do, our time is up for today anyway. So you take care and I'll be back to see you next week okay?'

Glynis had so much to work through, she couldn't wait to get back to her room and start making some notes. She had to try and piece together exactly what happened in her childhood, it was time for her to find her mother.

Chapter 30

Becky had been near death, not for the first time in her short life. Lukas's bullet had shattered her tiny shoulder and she was on a high dependency unit to manage and control bleeding. Her x-ray images had shown extensive breakage and although this wasn't life threatening, she wasn't likely to recover quickly.

Over time, Janette had discovered the absolute loneliness of this child and allocated one of her colleagues to take over her social work role. Amanda was South African, she was a force to be reckoned with and she loved children. She visited Becky every day and arranged for a foster couple to visit her too. Amanda was hoping to secure a long term foster placement for Becky when she came out of hospital.

One afternoon at visiting time, Becky had been moved to the children's general ward. Amanda and Janette, together with Rocco's input, had managed to sneak both Glynis and Layla in to the ward to see Becky.

It was amazing at how Becky perked up so quickly when she saw her two friends, the only friends she had ever really known. They couldn't stay long but the fact that they had visited at all was enough for the little girl to know she had hope.

'Here Becky, look we've got you your favourite chocolate.' beamed Glynis.

'Thank you, I love this.' replied Becky. They talked and giggled nervously about what had happened and how frightening it had been for all of them.

'The nurse said she will let me see Gilly if he is okay, he's in another ward, just down the corridor.' said Becky.

Gilly's injuries were rather more serious. His leg was broken in two places and his hand had been blown clean off by the bullet. The surgeon had managed to sew it back on. He would need hand therapy for at least twelve months, but he was alive and he was grateful for that.

Accompanied by Janette, Glynis and Layla manged to go to the ward where Gilly was recovering. He slept as they surrounded him. The silence of three highly energised women around his hospital bed awoke him with a start.

Although he was in incredible pain, he smiled at the sight of them.

'Oh it's you lot.' he exclaimed quietly, still smiling at them.

‘Hi Gilly, it’s good to see you, that bandage is huge.’ said Layla.

‘Can I write on the plaster cast on your leg?’ asked Glynis.

‘Go on then, you little minx, but don’t press too hard.’

They stayed for a while, long enough to watch Gilly drift back into a deep sleep.

Chapter

31

Glynis had to get out of the safe house, somewhere where she could be alone. Everything that she was working through in her therapy sessions was building up inside her head and making her feel like she wanted to burst.

The blue wheelie bin was always put out on a Thursday evening and Glynis knew that Arnold unlocked the door before he went through the whole house emptying the bins from each room. She waited quietly in the downstairs bathroom. Hearing the sound of the door being unlocked, followed by his footsteps as he went up the wooden staircase. Glynis silently slipped out. She had taken a precaution and worn a Rasta cap to keep her braids tucked in and change her appearance slightly.

Making her way to a different cemetery, she knew she would find some peace and have time to think clearly. It was her therapy, her place of peace and empowerment.

It was an old grave yard that was combined with new shiny black engraved head stones. These must be for cremations she thought as she sat in amongst the old gravestones, the ground all around them was overgrown and uncared for. Glynis always thought how sad that was.

After the last therapy session, Glynis decided that she definitely wanted to find her mother, to talk to her. She wanted to find out what had made her turn to drink, was it Glynis that had wound her up so much. She needed to know for sure, why she had abandoned her like she did. She needed answers, she was sad and angry and Jules had told her that she deserved answers.

After giving herself almost an hour of solace, she left the cemetery with a new sense of a mission. She got back to the safe house and slipped into the back garden through the unusually unlocked back gate, before she was missed.

Melanie who was sat at the table in the garden, smiled and looked at her as if to say, where were you. Glynis shrugged it off and went inside for some food, smiling.

Once in her room she called Janette and asked if she would come and see her at the safe house.

After the usual meet and greet and wellbeing questions, Janette asked Glynis why she had called her and how she could help her.

‘I want to go and see my mother. Since doing this therapy with Jules, there are things I need to know about her.’ said Glynis.

‘Well, if it’s what you really want, I will make it my business to find out where she is now and set it up. Are you absolutely sure that this is what you want Glynis?’ answered Janette, silently pleading to herself for it not be the case.

‘Yes, it’s what I want.’ answered Glynis.

True to her word, Janette set up a meeting the following week at the Longways Centre, a sheltered housing unit for recovering alcoholics.

Janette accompanied her to the Centre but Glynis asked her to wait in the car, saying that she needed to do it on her own.

Janette was not happy and she told Glynis so, but she agreed to let her do this one thing on her own. She’d had to be a tough kid and dragging herself through the care system, trying to survive the abusive behaviours of others, she wasn’t doing too bad.

Glynis looked so calm and well dressed with her flawless skin and braids so beautifully done. She had started to look like a young woman and she was beautiful.

Marilyn’s top lip twisted and she spat as she snarled at Glynis and how beautiful she actually was. Droplets of bitter spit flew out from her toxic mouth as she screamed at her daughter.

'Who the fuck do you think you are, miss high and mighty? Think you're better than the rest of us do you? Well, let me tell you. You are and always have been a spoilt little bitch. You will get what's coming to you. I'm surprised you're not pregnant already you little whore.'

When Glynis smiled at her because she now knew the truth. She had needed to come to see her mother to be sure. She was sure now.

Marilyn hated seeing Glynis smile with her perfect teeth. How dare she smile at her, how dare she be anything other than a petrified child. She attacked Glynis in a fit of anger in the sitting room of her sheltered flat, launching at her with her chubby hand around the child's throat.

Glynis finally defended herself and took hold of a huge piece of Marilyn's hair. She pushed her to the ground in an attempt to try and stop her mother's violent rage. She was bigger and stronger than she was as a child and she sure as hell didn't have to put up with it anymore.

The shelter manager upon hearing the commotion, rushed in to stop the fighting and Glynis let go of her mother's hair. She said nothing as she left the room and walked out of the building and into Janette's awaiting car.

'What happened?' asked Janette.

'I don't want to talk about it.' replied Glynis as she stared out of the car window.

Chapter

32

When Glynis received the letter to appear in court for the assault on her mother she was quite terrified. She had never received a letter before, let alone such an official one.

Court Appearance

25th May 2019

Ms Glynis Solomon

C/o J. Baxter (Social Worker)
North Callachen County Council Social Services
County Hall
Callachen
CL1 2DT

Re: Case number: GH14899657

Case: (G. Solomon -vs- M. Solomon)

Dear Ms Solomon:

Your case has been set for jury trial on 18th June 2019 at 10:00hrs in the county courthouse, located at 235 Major Street in Callachen, North Yorkshire.

Your case is before Judge, Justice Tanya Parkes QC, who will be in courtroom 18A. You will find it most convenient to park at Shrifneys corner car park.

Judge, Justice Tanya Parkes QC's courtroom is located on the second floor. I will meet you in the foyer at 09:00hrs on the morning of the trial. You must plan to be present for this. A copy of this letter has been sent to Janette Baxter (Social Worker) and the DCI Rochelle Raven from the Galaxy Section of the Callachen Police force. Because of your age you will be accompanied by an appropriate adult at all times.

If you have any questions, please feel free to call.

Sincerely,

Jessop and Langley

Shelley Langton

01447 585869 (ext. 147)

Glynis had been accused of launching an attack on her old and frail mother in the flat of her sheltered housing accommodation. There had been no mention that Glynis had only been trying to defend herself against her mother's violence, just as she had from a very early age.

The impending court case continued to leave her full of anxiety. Janette and Rocco had worked together and arranged for Glynis to have a psychological assessment that might assist with the case. They thought and hoped it might help with the fact that she seemed to need to spend so much time in graveyards and in the company of the dead.

As Janette was heavily involved with Glynis, she helped her to read and re read the letter. Together they researched what could happen in such a case by comparing it with similar incidents that they found on the internet.

Glynis talked it over with Layla and they decided that she must just tell the truth, however much that hurt, she must be honest and true.

Chapter 33

Jules had arrived at the contact centre for the next therapy session. Glynis had agreed to work with some Art Therapy as suggested. Jules set out a trauma tapestry.

Glynis had always loved drawing so it was easy for her, but she preferred to do it at the sessions and leave the pictures with Jules.

Jules explained to her that it was a great exercise especially because she was so good at drawing. It was a natural route of expression. She continued to clarify how the trauma tapestry worked from beginning to end.

Glynis started to draw images from memories of her life, her earlier childhood, her own lived experience and from her own perspective. Jules had explained that it didn't need to be pieces of art, stick drawings would be absolutely fine, as long as they came from her own memories, thoughts and feelings. Giving her a way to express her deepest memories and feelings.

Over time, Jules and Glynis taped together pictures

that she had drawn and letters that she had written to various members of her family. There was one to the mother she remembered as being loving and kind and one to the later version her mother had become, once the drink had set in. Glynis worked well and was happy with and what they meant to her. She was curious as to what would happen with the tapestry once it was finished.

'Well, all you have to do, is keep drawing and writing and collecting anything that allows you to make up and express what you need to. Keep going until you've drawn everything that you feel is enough. Now that we have started to tape it all together, you will see how you've created the beginnings of your unique tapestry.' answered Jules.

'Oh, what do I do with it then?' asked Glynis.

'When you feel that it is finished, you need to find a safe place to set light to it. Suggestions might be to burn it in a metal bin or an incinerator. It is crucial that you save all of the ashes. I can help with this if you want me to discuss the actual burning with Janette or at the safe house?'

'What, just burn it and forget about it?' asked Glynis.

'Well, not exactly, once you have burned it and saved what's left. You and only you get to decide what to do with the ashes…here are some examples.

Put the ashes into a pot or into the earth and grow a plant so that something beautiful comes from something not so beautiful.
Put the ashes into a piece of muslin and tie to an air balloon and let it go, watch until it disappears out of sight.
Take the ashes in a box or an envelope to a significant place or to where the bad stuff happened and leave or scatter them there.
Put the ashes in the toilet, skip, rubbish dump anywhere that is significant.
Or anything that you think would suit you the most, but you have to get rid of them Glynis.' answered Jules.

As the therapeutic process continued, Glynis had continued to work through her psychological tapestry of what had been uncovered in her guided visualisation.

She was still reeling from what she had learned, she had kept to herself and was unable to tell anyone at all. As a counsellor, Jules had to adhere to a strict set of rules, ethics and boundaries but Glynis promised that she would disclose it herself, she just needed some time and space to think about it.

Glynis began a new journey of understanding for one so young and in doing so, she began a slow path towards post traumatic growth.

Jules had explained in more detail so that it was easily understandable, that what Glynis did when she left her body was called dissociation. She told her that not only was it more common than not, it was almost a regular part of a clients' recollection of their survival of the abusive behaviours of others.

Jules had asked her at one session to observe some of her memories as her dissociated self, looking down on the terror of what she had been subjected to. As her dissociated self, she could relate and respond to Jules in a different way and she was able to engage at a much deeper and more intense level. As well as that, there seemed to be no emotion involved.

Jules gently suggested for Glynis to imagine and visualise a powerful animal of her choice, and to take that chosen animal with her to revisit the worst traumatic incident in her early years.

Glynis was enthralled by this new way of communication, Jules explained that by bypassing the emotional element, the information was able to get passed into the memory bank, where it could be stored naturally into the brains filing system. She made sense of why and how Glynis was able to adapt to and conclude their work a lot more safely and efficiently.

Glynis understood all of this information far more efficiently than any adult that Jules had ever worked with.

It made sense to Jules too because such a way of working was even more resourceful if the client was sufficiently relaxed as in trance state, just like when they had done the guided visualisation work.

Chapter 34

Raymond Solomon had decided to look for his daughter. It could have been the deep seated guilt that ran through his veins, for the horror that he knew he had caused his only child.

Or, it could have been the phone call he received out of the blue from a Lithuanian man called Lukas, offering him money to bring his daughter to him.

Raymond admitted to himself that he often wondered what happened to his only daughter. His wife Marilyn was too far gone and hardly ever sober enough to talk to him. She had her own life with her pathetic, drunken cronies in the shelter where she lived. He was still free from such complete intoxication and hadn't touched drugs for more than four years.

Funny, he thought, as he walked through his local park to watch the children. The day after he had received the call from Lukas offering him the money to find his daughter, he also received a WhatsApp message from

Marilyn saying how the kid had been to her flat and beaten her up and how she was going to take her to court.

There was an inane curiosity attached to this and he needed to find out what was really going on. He knew how abusive and violent Marilyn could be and had mostly turned a blind eye to it when the kid was younger.

He was angry at himself and his own weakness. He hated how he always gave in to his depravities, just a bit of fiddling he thought. He never seriously hurt any children. He wondered what Glynis might look like now, she must be at least thirteen he thought.

He also wondered what he could do with ten thousand pounds, maybe put a deposit on a flat, even get a little driving job.

He had no idea where to start to look for Glynis except to maybe contact social services in Callachen. She was his daughter after all, and he had parental rights.

Chapter

35

Janette called at the safe house and sent Arnold a quick message from her car, to get the all clear before going to the door.

'Do you want a cuppa?' called Melanie from the kitchen, as Janette, Layla and Glynis sat in the living room.

'I'd love one Mel, thanks.' answered Janette.

'Can I talk with Glynis alone?' Janette asked Layla.

'No, I want her to stay, we make decisions together.' said Glynis.

'Okay, if you're sure. It's okay with me. So, what I've come about Glynis, is that your father has been in touch and wants to see you. He says that he still has parental rights and has a right to know that you are well, happy and okay.' replied Janette.

Glynis suddenly started to breathe fast, with short sharp raspy breaths. Layla and Janette could see that she was going into a severe panic attack. Layla quickly ran into the kitchen and grabbed a paper bag from a drawer. Screwing the top to make a breathing hole, she sat with Glynis and got her to breathe gently into the bag, in and out. In and out.

'That's it Glyn, you know what to do?' soothed Layla, gently rubbing Glynis's back as she took instructions and breathed into the bag.

'Okay, that's it mate, a couple more breaths without the bag.' continued Layla.

Janette watched the bravery of these two young girls, their unbreakable bond and complete devotion to each other as they sat working through what most adults would have no idea about.

'Shall I leave you to it and come back tomorrow?' asked Janette.

'No, tell me what he said and what he wants, I am not going to live with him ever. Do you understand that? I would rather kill myself.' answered Glynis, through a recovery of panicked breathing.

'Okay, well, he just wants to meet to see how you are and if you are happy, well, that's what he says anyway.' answered Janette.

'I think it might be a good thing Glynis, but you must not go alone. I mean look what happened when you went to see your mother?' said Layla.

'I think I'd like to go because I have some questions for him, questions that I can't ask him when anyone else is there. And I'm definitely not going to live with him, not ever.' repeated Glynis.

Within two weeks, Janette had instigated an agreement, in part set up by Social Services with herself and the Galaxy Unit.

Glynis was only just fourteen, going on forty, as Janette liked to comment. She was still a child in the eyes of the law. The meeting was to be held at the contact centre. The same centre as where she had received her therapy.

It was in a different room and there was a two way mirror/glass in situ for protection, because Glynis had insisted on having some privacy with her father.

They were being observed by Rocco and Mark so that Glynis would be completely safeguarded. Glynis had agreed to allow Janette to sit in on the meeting but to sit at the edge of the room, away from them.

Raymond arrived at the contact centre first and was taken to the meeting room. He tapped his fingers on the table driving himself mad with anxiety.

'Dad.' said Glynis quietly, as she entered the room with Janette.

'Wow! Look at you, my baby girl, so grown up. So beautiful. You got a hug for your Dad?'

'I don't hug.' replied Glynis, as she sat opposite her father at a carefully placed table.

'Okay, okay that's alright. How are you?' asked Raymond.

'I'm good, really good. Why are you here after all this time. What do you want?' answered Glynis, puzzled.

'I got to thinking, you know, it's been such a long time and I'm sober and clean from any drugs. I thought perhaps we could think about building a relationship. Maybe I could finally take care of my little girl?' answered Raymond.

'Are you for real? I've practically bought myself up. Why would I want to live with you? Dad, I know what you fucking did. It's all here in my memory and I tell you now. It won't be long before I tell the whole world what you did to me.' replied Glynis, her anger palpable.

Raymond looked at his daughter in disbelief, he wasn't quite sure what she was referring to, was it the fiddling at night time, when he read her a story. Or was it something else. He held his head in his hands.

'I need a toilet break.' said Glynis.

The pregnant pause gave way to a moment of pure craving as Mark and Rocco were sat very close together. He gently touched her face with his hand and they shared a soft kiss. Seeing the child return they stopped.

'It will wait.' said Mark

They both adjusted themselves and returned to watching the strange reunion between Glynis and her father.

'I'm so sorry Glynis, I really am baby girl. I'm sorry I was such a shit Dad and I'm sorry that you have been through such a rough time of it. But look at you now, you are beautiful. I can't believe how you've grown up so much.'

'I'm only where I am because that excuse for a mother argued with the truancy officer and this woman here, she is a social worker. It was her who saved me, not you and I have a life ahead of me that I am not going to let you ruin again. Now tell me the truth about why you are really here?'

Raymond was quite frightened of his daughter, gone was the needy, little, loving kid with the big crazy afro hair that couldn't be tamed. Now, here in front of him, sat a young woman, not taking any shit. Beautifully presented and with brass balls, just like her mother.

'Truth is, I had a call from a man asking me to find you for him. At first I was interested in the money, I'll be honest. But now, now that I've seen you. I really do want to get to know you again. Honestly baby girl, I really do.' said Raymond, tears streaming down his face.

'There it is, I knew it was too good to be true.' replied Glynis, sarcastically. She banged the palms of her hands on the table.

'Baby girl, listen to me. I'm just trying to be honest with you is all. You can't be vexed about that, it's what you want isn't it?' pleaded Raymond.

'Janette, I need to get out of here. I've had enough.' exclaimed Glynis, getting up to leave.

Raymond begged her to stay, he tried to grab her hand across the table and she pushed him away.

Mark was on the ball, instantly after hearing their conversation about a man looking for his daughter. As Janette guided Glynis out of the room, he was standing at the door to stop Raymond from leaving.

'If you could just wait here a minute Sir, we have some questions?' said Mark.

'You can't keep me here man, I am not under arrest?'

'Mr Solomon, I am arresting you for the suspicion of child trafficking and serious child neglect. Is that better Sir?' said Rocco, as she stood behind Mark.

'We can do this here, right now, or we can take you back to the station. Your choice?' said Mark.

'Oh for fuck sake, let's do it now, but I haven't done anything like trafficking as you call it, I don't know what you're on about.' replied Raymond.

'We just want to know who the bloke is who has asked you to find your daughter Mr Solomon. Just tell us that and we will let you go.' asked Rocco.

'All I know is that his name is Lukas, he is foreign and he offered me ten grand to find my daughter and bring her to him.' answered Raymond.

'You were going to do that to your own daughter?' asked Mark, the disbelief evident, across his face.

‘Yes, but once I met her and seen how she’s grown up so much. I couldn’t have done that. I was stupid, I don’t know what I was thinking.’ replied Raymond.

‘Do you have this man’s contact details?’ asked Rocco.

Raymond reached into his pocket for his mobile phone and searched the contacts list. There under the name Lith-Lukas was the contact they were looking for, he read out the number.

Mark took down the number and left the room momentarily, giving him enough time to ring it in to the unit for Nate to act on it and follow up the lead.

Chapter

36

The final session with Jules had been hard for Glynis, she had never met anyone like her. Someone who listened to her and was even interested in her story, her young lived experience. She would be sorry to say goodbye but knew it was time.

They had both reached as far as they could go and Glynis had learned so much throughout the therapy sessions. Not only answering so many questions in her repressed memory bank. But helping her with her self-esteem, working with responses to unkindness and a whole set of mindfulness techniques to support her with future issues.

Jules had asked her at their last session, to bring something that signified an ending for her, something that she might always remember.

Glynis had bought a jam jar full of different coloured glass chippings. She readily admitted that she had collected them for as long as she could remember and wanted Jules to have them to prove her fondness for her and to say thank you for being so cool all the time.

Later that day, watched by a protection officer, Glynis sat in the huge tyre that swung gently to and fro, as it hung from the giant oak tree at the back of the safe house.

After her long and intense therapy sessions, her young brain was still processing what she had uncovered. She was trying to put the pieces together. She knew what she had to do, she knew what she had discussed again and again with Jules but had still been unable to tell her everything.

Right now, she couldn't even tell Layla what was going on in her head. It was just too sad, too much for her to bear, let alone to burden her best friend with.

Distracted by the Court case that seemed to loom closer and closer, Glynis thought about how the clinical psychologist would assess her and whether or not she might send her away, away from everything and everyone she loved.

Not for the first time in her short life Glynis considered ending her life, it was too hard. Every corner was another fight. If she hadn't had Layla she would have done it a long time ago. But she and her friend had plans to get far away, she would never let her down, not now. Not when they were so close to their dream.

Chapter

37

'What was that back there?' asked Rocco.

'What this?' replied Mark as he leant in to kiss Rocco again.

Their embrace was passionate and neither could resist as they enjoyed one another's touch. A beautiful, clandestine connection. 'Back to my place?' asked Mark softly.

'I'll drive, answered Rocco, smiling. Marks place was immaculate, no sooner were they in the door, than they were both almost naked, clothes strewn across the floor, leaving a trail towards his bedroom.

Gently breathing and enjoying that pause of time after an hour of pure passion, Mark gently stroked Rocco's bare skin as he watched her relaxing in the bed next to him.

'I've wanted you for so long, do you know that?' said Mark.

'Yes, I do know that, you've not exactly hidden it?' smiled Rocco.

Mark took in her jet black hair, pale skin and emerald green eyes, which were delicately enhanced by the white cotton sheet barely covering her. In silence they lay, just content with being together in the early hours before the chaos and madness was bound to ensue.

Mark was interested in every single bit of information about her. What she was like as a child, what made her join the job, her siblings and how she lived now in a rambling old windmill? He wanted to know about Albie and he wanted to know what her life had been like with her ex-husband Mike. He could have listened to her all day and all night.

Rocco told him about her parents and the wordless love that she still felt for them, how she thought about them every single day. She told him how sad life was without them and how they were snatched away too soon. It had nearly broken the family, the siblings who were left. Conrad her brother was the glue that held them all together now. Her doctor at the time had said she was possibly mentally ill and signed her off work for three months.

'What did you do when you found out they had died?' asked Mark.

'I broke. I completely lost it for a while, my brother Conrad helped no end. The doctor gave me some tablets, but they just made me feel really sick and much worse.' replied Rocco, a solitary tear just dampened her right eye. He noticed how it glistened. He listened intently, watching her speak. The light from the street lamp emphasised her beauty, while all around them silence echoed in Marks spacious Victorian apartment.

'Well, it sounds to me like you were probably grieving rather than actually being mentally ill and that just maybe, the medication you had been given might actually have made you feel worse than you were, increasing your sadness. These medications can sometimes completely mess people up.' said Mark assuring her with a wink and a smile that he was no doctor.

'Now you stay there, I'm going to make us some food.' said Mark, full of excitement at finally getting the woman of his dreams all to himself. He knew it would be fleeting. He knew he couldn't have her forever, but while he did, he was going to make sure she was happy.

Rocco got up just after him, with the sheet still wrapped around her like a sari. Finding the bathroom, she gently looked around the magnificent room. Mirrors adorned one complete wall. She admired the expensive looking men's hair and body moisturisers, his bath oils looked exquisite. She read the label, screwing her eyes up. Trying to read with no glasses was getting more and more difficult. The first one called Bergamot Balm Oil read;

"*A sensual bathing oil enriched with nourishing Caribbean papaya seeds for divine softness. This majestic bath oil will enhance your skin with its alluring tea tree, jojoba, coconut oil, raspberry seeds and bergamot. Let it soothe away the aches and stresses of the day as you soak in its warm oil and stress freeing glory.*"

Unscrewing the lid to sniff, she felt like the cat who had got the cream. Her, a detective chief inspector had single handedly found the source of Mark Walsh's gorgeous aroma. Everyone talked about it at work and she, she had found it. She giggled to herself as she found her way back to the kitchen.

He had such good taste, she thought to herself. The kitchen was a mixture of deep and interesting matt colours, there was a deep ochre, which reminded her of English mustard. The doors were all painted in black chalk paint, it surprised and impressed her in equal measure. She could see that he had carefully chosen all the pots, pans and crockery to match.

'Did you renovate this place Mark?' asked Rocco with interest.

'Yes. Most of it, my old man helped where he could. He was good at finding simple ways to refresh a cooking space. He was also a delicious cook. Are you warm enough?' replied Mark.

Rocco nodded and smiled. She loved looking around this huge kitchen. He had accumulated a stylish mix of accessories, a set of black leather stools, the lighting was gentle, the cabinets were painted to perfection and the aroma of whatever he was cooking was making her mouth water.

Moving around the kitchen island to take Rocco a glass of red wine, he cupped her face with one huge hand and they kissed passionately. Rocco suddenly pulled away at exactly the same time as he did, they both laughed at the hissing sound of water, boiling over onto the flame of the cooker ring.

'Bloody pasta!' exclaimed Mark, smiling at a laughing Rocco. She watched as he chopped tomatoes, he talked as he added onion and garlic and nonchalantly let them gently cook on their own. Effortlessly keeping an eye on everything whilst entertaining Rocco with anecdotes of his childhood.

'Do you always make your own pasta sauce Mark, I get mine from the supermarket?' asked Rocco, captivated by his culinary prowess.

Mark smiled at her as he strained the pasta into the sink. He pretended to be a top chef with an attempt at a French accent, the feeble effort of which, made Rocco spit some of her wine out onto the worktop. It was very unladylike but neither cared as they laughed together.

'Please, Madam, follow me to your table if you will?' gestured Mark, bowing, with a tea towel over one forearm and the other hand pointing to another area in the apartment.

Smiling, Rocco followed him to yet another impressive room. She took in the rich vibrant colours and wondered when he had found the time to set the table.

Even the napkins were a kind of African orange, tinged with sunset red.

Mark laid the food out on the table, they ate and talked and laughed until there was just enough time to go back to bed and try and get some serious sleep before work.

The buzzing of a phone woke them both as they unlocked their bodies from each other.

'Yes, who, what, what is it?' asked Mark?'

'Why are you answering Rocco's phone Mark?' replied a woman's voice, who, through his slightly hungover tiredness, he vaguely recognised as Stacey.

Mark gestured a forefinger across his neck to stop Rocco from talking. He hadn't realised that he'd picked up the wrong phone because the ring tones were the same.

'Oh, she left it in my car last call yesterday. I'm just going to pop it round to her before I come in. I think she's interviewing at social services today isn't she?' answered Mark.

‘Yes, I’m supposed to be with her but funnily enough Mark, I can’t get an answer at hers. Don’t worry though, I’m sure she’ll rock up soon enough. Catch you later mate?’ replied Stacey clicking to end the phone call.

‘Shit! Do you think they know I’m here?’ asked Rocco.

‘Does it really matter Roc, I mean how could you honestly resist me for this long, everyone knows that you’re madly in love with me?’ joked Mark, smiling.

Rocco playfully slapped him on the shoulder. ‘I suppose so, although we both know it’s completely the other way around, but I’ll let you dream on. Can I get a shower?’

‘Yes help yourself, I’ll get you some different shower gel though, or it really will give it away.’

Mark found some lemon fizz shower gel that his sister had left the last time she visited. While Rocco showered he made the bed, cleaned the bedroom and gathered up the clothes from the night before. He carefully laid hers out so that they were ready for her and then hurried her up as they passed in the shower as she got out.

‘That’s called frotteurism you know. We can’t touch bodies, we’ll mix the scents Mark.’ laughed Rocco rushing back into the bedroom, leaving him to shower on his own.

As he walked back into the bedroom, she admired his strong muscular physique. His skin colour was just beautiful and the light reflected on the shine of his muscles as he got dressed. His dreadlocks were flawless. He caught her looking and smiled.

'See, you just cannot resist me, can you?'

'I was just looking at your dreadlocks actually. How on earth do they look so cool? I mean, all the bloody time man. Now come on, I'll have to drive you back to your car first. Then I have to get home and make some calls. We can catch up later?' answered Rocco.

As they drove to pick up his car, Mark could sense himself starting to feel miserable. He didn't want to live his life without this woman ever, and he had absolutely no idea how to play it now that their night was over. He was torn, should he just be grateful for the time they had just spent together or should he continue to pursue her.

'Shall we try and catch up tomorrow night?' said Rocco unexpectedly, as she parked next to his car.

Mark stared at her as if she had just slapped him. He was instantaneously taken aback. Never in his dreams did he expect a second date, if it could be called that.

'Yes, well, I'll have to check my calendar. Joking, I'm joking, I'll cancel anything and everything for you,

you beautiful creature.' answered Mark, smiling and very happy.

Chapter

38

Lukas Baltakis's arrest had led to a further seven associated members of the same organised crime gang to be detained. They had been running a child sexual exploitation ring within Callachen Town and the surrounding areas.

Johnno and Fitz had been procured by the eight men to find girls and to carefully build an emotional connection with them. Johnno had gained Glynis's trust and in doing so he was able to procure her for sex with the men, preparing her for a world where they would be trafficked into much worse.

At the Plea and Trial Preparation Hearing, the men from three different countries pleaded guilty as the full accounts of their crimes were read out. The men had exploited girls as young as ten and were likely to be given sentences ranging from five to twenty two years.

Earlier, whilst taking his statement, Lukas had also been accused of two rapes, aiding and abetting gang rape, sexual assault of girls under thirteen and trafficking for the purposes of sexual exploitation. He was likely to be given an additional sentence of up to nineteen years in prison. His dream of returning to his French haven was slowly ebbing away.

Before these men had been arrested, Nate and Ruth had done the groundwork to ensure they would remain in custody until a court hearing date could be given. An assessment had to be undertaken by the Callachen local authority to work alongside and in close co-operation with the (MSHTU) Modern Slavery Human Trafficking Unit. Immigration staff who were familiar with patterns of trafficking into and out of the UK.

The safe house provision was already in place so that both girls could give full disclosure and information about their circumstances. Their location had been kept quiet apart from the Galaxy Unit and Immigration Services.

As more information was disclosed by each of the girls. It became evident that the extended grooming of them and many more like them, had involved exploitative situations, contexts and mock relationships where they head received something good as a 'reward' such as an introduction to drugs, alcohol, cigarettes, affection, gifts and money as a result of them performing, and/or another or others performing on them, sexual activities. Violence, coercion and intimidation being all too common.

The Galaxy Unit were fully aware that any involvement in exploitative relationships was often characterised by the child's or young person's limited availability of choice as a result of their damaged home life and their total emotional vulnerability.

Glynis nor Layla, although suspicious at first, had not recognised the coercive nature of what they had perceived as a genuine boyfriend/girlfriend type relationship. Layla especially, did not see herself as a victim and Glynis was deeply embarrassed and reactive to be given such a title.

They had no idea that what they were going through was classed as being groomed or sexually exploited. They didn’t understand how the risk to them had been heightened because of the fact that they were in care.

When watching the hearing Nate sat with Ruth. He told her about how children going through this kind of neglect and what he called abandonment didn’t stand a chance.

‘The thing is Ruth, these girl know that there is another life, another way to live, they know it exists but because the parenting they receive is so poor, they have no way of knowing or experiencing any other way of being. It’s a sad truth, but it happens and I should know. I’ve seen no end of it.’ said Nate with a deep sadness.

Chapter

39

Was it a sense of foreboding, or a knowing of what was to come maybe? Nobody will ever know or understand why Raymond Solomon took fifty two Tramadol mixed with enough Ketamine and whiskey to kill a horse, as he lay in the filthy apartment he had come to call home.

He had written two letters, one was to Marilyn telling her what a whore she was and how he wished he had never laid eyes on her. The other was just a scrawny note for Glynis which said,

"Glyn, I am so sorry, I really am. I know you saw what happened and I can't live knowing that. You are a beautiful kid. I hope you find all that you are looking for. I hope you find the truth, because it will set you free." Love Dad x

His funeral was a small affair and Glynis was permitted to attend with Hesh and Stacey, She didn't get too close because Marilyn was also there and she didn't want her to cause another scene or say that Glynis was being violent towards her again. She couldn't take another lie, another court case. She didn't want to fight anymore.

Chapter

40

The court day finally arrived and it was heard in Court 18A of the Callachen Crown Court as the letter had stated it would be. The case details were read out.

Glynis Louise Solomon who was of no fixed abode, when the incident occurred shortly before 2pm on Friday 11th August 2018

After being attacked by the victim, Ms Solomon claimed that she acted in self-defence.

The victim known as Marilyn Solomon sustained head and facial injuries as a result of the altercation before fleeing into a nearby neighbouring housing unit.

Other charges to be brought before the court were four separate incidents of grave robbing.

Glynis had chosen to speak for herself after the long discussions that she had engaged in with Jules.

As she stood in the witness box after Marilyn had given her evidence, she looked around the court and saw Jules in the public gallery with Layla and Janette. She smiled nervously at them.

She was also shocked but delighted to see the familiar face of Tilly Shepherd, her childhood neighbour, the one who had taken care of her earlier on in her life. Janette had kept in touch with her over the years and was keeping her up to speed with her mother and the toxic relationship.

Rocco, Stacey, Hesh and Mark from the Galaxy Unit were in the inner circle, in a row to themselves and their eyes never left Glynis's as she coughed to clear her throat ready to speak.

There were the normal twelve jurors who she tried not to look at, at all.

'Ms Solomon can you tell us why, on four separate occasions that we know of. You dug up the freshly covered graves of Mrs Lillian Alconby, Mr Robert Duvall, Mr Arnold Briggson and Mrs Millicent Thackard at both Marsh Lane Cemetery and the Callachen All Saints Cemetery?' asked the prosecution solicitor, Mr Rogerson.

'I was searching for my mother.' answered Glynis.

'Your mother Ms Solomon, resides at 17 The Plough Units, Callachen Fields, Callachen. What a load of poppy cock, could you not have just gone to that address if you had wanted to see her.' said Mr Rogerson, for the prosecution, as he shook his head, puffing out his rotund, salad dodging midriff.

'Come, come now, what is this farcical attempt at misleading us all again?' he continued, indignantly.

Staring straight ahead, Glynis took a deep breath as she began her own defence.

'Marilyn is not my mother, she pretends that she is but her real name is Patricia Betts.'

The court was plummeted into silence, you really could have heard a pin drop in that courtroom..

'Again this is more rubbish to make us and the members of the jury believe that you are the victim here, that you are innocent, just more and more lies.' bawled Mr Rogerson.

Layla and Janette sat transfixed as Glynis told her truth. Jules smiled as she watched this beautiful, strong young woman, for once in her life, have a voice. It was a voice that shook, but it was a strong and truthful voice.

Still staring straight ahead, Glynis continued,

'My mother is buried under the garage at 37 Church View near Callachen Heights. My father killed her and cut off her head, I saw it happen but I had buried it way down in my memory. I think I've been searching for her ever since, that's why I go to graveyards, trying to find her.'

Glynis showed no emotion as she spoke about the knowledge she had, as she relayed the information to the court.

'Is this really relevant your honour, the defendant is clearly trying to fabricate a multitude of lies in what little time we have left.' argued the brusque, bearded barrister.

'Of course it's relevant Mr Rogerson, objection overruled and we have as much time as it takes, please carry on Ms Solomon.' Said the Judge.

There were gasps and wonders amidst the overwhelming silence.

The Judge, Justice Tanya Parkes QC, held up her hand and said,

'Silence in court'. she looked directly at the young girl in the dock as if there were just the two of them in the courtroom.

Compassion filled her eyes and her heart as she said gently,

'Are you telling the court Ms Solomon, that, as a child, you have witnessed the murder of your mother and that you have information and evidence of that murder?'

'Yes your honour, I am.' said Glynis, she was still staring ahead, but had changed direction to look straight at the Judge.

'Okay, Ms Solomon, I am going to adjourn the court for two weeks while the police talk with you to get this information and evidence substantiated. Then we will see what happens from there. Does that sound okay to you?'

'Thank you your honour, and thank you for listening to me.' answered Glynis, politely.

Every person in that courtroom who knew Glynis, was not only in shock, but in awe of her strength and courage at what she had kept hidden for so long. All thinking to themselves no doubt, that is was no wonder she stopped speaking when she was so young. No wonder she spent so long in graveyards.

Her subconscious must have known that her mother was below the ground.

Chapter 41

Janette had become really attached to Glynis and Layla. She had no idea of the amount of money that they had hidden away and so she donated an old iPad to Layla so that she could do some research as they carried on their schooling from the safe house. Some of their education was formally tailored to suit their needs online and they were also allowed to have a teacher to come in twice a week.

Just before the court case, Layla got to thinking about her own mother. She hadn't received anything from her in a while. Contact had been sporadic to say the least but in her heart she still felt very much loved by her mother.

Layla was actually a whizz with any kind of device. She was so grateful to Janette, she had been Glynis's only constant since being taken into care and it was obvious how much she loved the girl. Glynis didn't quite trust Janette because she could have her moved in a heartbeat but she felt safe with her, to a point.

Layla was able to access an old email address that she hadn't been able to get into for a couple of years. With plenty of time to kill, she trawled through each one, pressing delete every millisecond. Amongst the hundreds of spam emails in the inbox, she noticed one that looked like it might be genuine.

It was from an Australian solicitor called Oliver Jenson. Her mother and long term boyfriend (who she had never met) had been jailed after a road traffic collision. Her mother's house had been passed to Layla under a law called Temporarily Assignment of Assets to a Loved One. All of her mother's assets had been transferred to her. It read to her that Layla was now responsible to take care of her mother's obligations during her time in prison. The solicitor also laid out the fact that once the assets had been transferred to Layla, she was not obligated to return such assets when her mother was free to leave prison.

There had been no legal document drawn up to say that she would have to give it back and Layla thought that this meant the house must be hers. She wasn't happy about being made to go to Australia though.

The email also stated that a sum of two hundred thousand Australian dollars had also been assigned to her to help with the mortgage and the upkeep of the property. This was far more than her and Glynis already had squirrelled away.

Two weeks previously, the girls had gone into town where they were supposed to be at the cinema. Accompanied by a protection officer, who waited outside, they managed to sneak out of the fire door and back in before the film ended.

Researching banks on the internet, they wanted an account that was accessible online from anywhere in the world. The instructions said that they had to set up a student bank account and deposit the cash. The cashier had asked lots of questions and Layla had given her mother's details for everything. Her being abroad explained why they had so much money. They knew it would be safer in a bank account and apart from the questions at first. There didn't seem to be any problem.

Within twenty four hours they were sent the account details.

The email from the solicitor contained four other attachments. Layla opened them one by one. The first was how to access prison visiting orders, it was a huge document. It explained the first visit, how there was a system in place that she would need to log in to each time. There was a one hundred point identification check that she would have to go through as well as to provide certain documentation. Each set of identification accrued a different number of points. She had grasped the concept but decided that she would look at that later.

The second attachment was about how many of the Australian prison services use a bio metric enrolment system.

This would mean that they would need to take her fingerprints on the first visit. This too, was overwhelming and so she thought she would leave that until later as well. Until she could find someone to help her with this whole email.

She kept looking, the third email was a copy of part of the newspaper report from what had happened in the road that day.

"An English mother will spend more than twelve years behind bars after a shocking road collision which killed four people. Two of those who died were in separate vehicles and the other two were merely passers-by who died on impact.

Emergency services were called to a three-vehicle collision around 15:30hrs on Sunday at Mullacombe Road, Rock Hallington, just outside of Rockhampton.

Queensland Police Assistant Commissioner Michael Larkin, told reporters it was a tragedy that can never be forgotten. He stated, "It was a sad day, and has resulted in four lives being lost

Mr Nigel Bunce, said witnesses and first responders were confronted with an "extremely cataclysmic sight. Despite the incredible efforts of witnesses and later Queensland Ambulance Service, both drivers and pedestrians died at the scene.

Police have charged Pippa Anderson with dangerous driving. She was also four times over the legal limit for alcohol consumption."

Layla cried when she saw a photograph of her mother having been arrested. There was also a courtroom sketch of her mother in the court dock. She looked terrified in both.

The last attachment was a scanned image of a note from her mother that she had given to the solicitor to pass on to her daughter.

"Dear Layla,

My beautiful daughter, I'm so sorry to have to write this letter at such a bad time. I am fully guilty of killing those people. I didn't get up and out of bed that day with an intention to kill anyone. But look, it's happened and I am doing the time. Even time in prison won't bring those people back and I will not be able to live with myself whether I'm in prison or released at any time in the future. I don't care what happens to me now, I deserve every bit of it.

You though, my delightful daughter, I want you to have a good start. The house is yours and you can sell it and set yourself up in the UK or come over to Australia and make a new start here. I don't know what's going on with you right now but now is my chance to finally make you happy. Oliver Jensen will take care of everything. He is being well paid to keep the house and anything else that needs sorting, in order.

He will be there to meet you when you arrive, if you choose to come over.

Please don't hate me darling. Take your time to go through this letter and everything that I've instructed Oliver to send you. Speak to someone you know, get advice. Write to me when you can, okay. Remember how much I love you. You are and always will be, forever in my heart.

Love as Always

Mum

Xxx

Layla closed the email and went to wash her face. Glynis was waiting for her in the kitchen.

'You okay mate?' asked Glynis.

'No I'm not but listen, we'll talk about it later when we go to bed alright. Everything okay with you?' replied Layla.

Chapter

42

Knocking on the blue door of number 37 Church View, Rocco and Mark were greeted by Mr and Mrs Hilliard and their little dog 'Marlon.'

Holding up their police identity cards, Rocco introduced them.

'Hello, I'm DCI Rochelle Raven and this is my colleague PC Mark Walsh. I wonder if we can come in for a moment to talk with you?'

'What is this about, what have we done, what's going on?' asked Mrs Hilliard, as she tried to calm the little dog from barking and jumping up.

'Let me put him out in the other room and I'll be back. Can I get you a cup of tea or anything?' asked Mr Hilliard.

'Oh I would love one please if that's okay, tea, with milk and two sugars for me please and DCI Raven has coffee, black?' said Mark eagerly.

Rocco didn't say anything as she smiled, raising her eyebrows discreetly towards him. She was a bit taken aback that he remembered how she liked her coffee.

When the Hilliard's were sat back down and the dog was safely locked away. Rocco began.

'Okay so, no one is any trouble, we would just like to take some details about when you purchased this house and any information you can give us, as to previous owners. And then we would like to have a look around the outside. There is a possibility I'm afraid, that we might need to dig up some of your back yard.' Explained Rocco.

'Dig up my plants, are you mad inspector?' exclaimed Mr Hilliard.

'Why do you want our garden, oh my word, what have we been living on?' said Mrs Hilliard as the little dog continued its relentless yapping from the other side of the glass door.

'We have evidence to suggest that between eleven and thirteen years ago, a serious crime was committed at this property. We need to find out of that is true. The only way we can do that Mr and Mrs Hilliard, is to excavate the earth beneath your double garage. Look, I will personally ensure that every piece of earth that we have to excavate is replaced as good as new. Now, this may take some time, but I can assure you that it will be done.' answered Rocco, as encouragingly as she could.

‘Well, I’ll be damned, you hear about this sort of thing, but you never think it will happen to you!’ said Mr Hilliard.

‘When will you start?’ asked Mrs Hilliard.

‘We would ideally like to start immediately, as early as tomorrow.’ answered Mark.

‘How long is this going to take?’ asked Mr Hilliard.

‘Please don’t worry, either of you. Our forensic archaeologists are experts at this, they do it all the time. They will be in and out in a few days and then we will leave you in peace. answered Rocco.

‘Well, what if I don’t want you to go digging up my garden?’ said Mr Hilliard, indignantly.

‘I’m afraid we have the legal authority Sir, this is a serious crime, a murder investigation. It’s bang in the middle of a crown court case and has been ordered by the Judge.’ replied Mark.

‘Have you got anywhere you can go and stay, just while they get on with it?’ asked Rocco, trying desperately to appease the Hilliard’s.

Mr Hilliard, who by this time, was pacing the floor, was becoming more and more agitated. Mrs Hilliard was getting irritated by him.

‘Oh do sit down David, let’s try and help if we can?’ said Mrs Hilliard.

'Look, here are mine and DCI Raven's contact details. We'll be back with the excavation team tomorrow.

Let us know if you have any questions or if there's anything we can do to help beforehand. We'll leave you in peace now and give you time to digest this information, but we would really appreciate your cooperation with this.' said Mark.

'Okay, thank you for that, we appreciate it, we will be in touch if we need to.' replied Mr Hilliard, who was slowly beginning to grasp the urgency of the matter.

Mark and Rocco got up to leave and Mrs Hilliard saw them to the door.

'Don't mind him, he would fall out with himself if he could. It will be okay, you do what you have to do.' said Mrs Hilliard

They both sat for a moment in silence, staring ahead as they let the heightened energy of the Hilliard's leave them.

'Come on, let's go and get a decent coffee from that Italian Tuscan Café, I'm buying.' said Mark.

Chapter

43

Stacey and Rocco arrived at the Brooke Clinic ten minutes early. Jules was setting up for the day and said she had to quickly take a phone call. She invited them to take a seat in the waiting room and to help themselves to a hot drink from a machine in the corner of the room that whirred and churned its contents, emitting a warm and creamy aroma of real fresh coffee.

As they waited, enjoying their coffee, they both observed the richness of the clinic, looking around at the high ceilings and large rooms. It must have been an old house, converted to a medical building thought Stacey.

'Hi, I'm ready now and I'm sorry to have kept you waiting. I had to take a phone call and these General Practitioners you know, they just won't wait!' exclaimed Jules, flicking her hair back from her face.

'That's okay, thank you for seeing us. You know that I'm DCI Rochelle Raven and this is my colleague, Sergeant Stacey Lord.' said Rocco holding out her hand to Jules.

'Yes we have met at some of the TAC meetings. So, how can I help you today?' asked Jules.

'We'd like to ask you some questions about one of your younger clients from the Heartsholme Children's Home. Her name is Glynis Solomon.'

'Look, you know I can't disclose confidential information about clients and/or the work we do, but I will help where I can.' answered Jules.

'We understand that, we just want to know if she has engaged with you, has she been open and honest and has anything come up that we might need to know about. I mean, she is still a minor and surely you have a duty of care to disclose anything that may bring or cause her harm. Anything of a safeguarding nature?' asked Stacey.

'She has engaged really well, she is always on time and totally respects the time she has in the therapy room. She has worked well with all interventions asked of her and has a good understanding of her life to date. We have worked with talking therapy, I have used interventions such as guided visualisation, a trauma tapestry programme and we're currently working on an ending. We have booked a session for when the court case is all over. I am fully aware of the court case and how this has taken up a lot of her thinking time. It's kind of stopped any other work for now, to be honest.' replied Jules.

'Okay well that's good to know and to have an idea of what's happening for her. Has Glynis ever talked about hurting herself or had suicidal thoughts?' asked

Rocco, completely ignoring the confidentiality breach that Jules had just mentioned.

Jules made a sort of well I want to tell you but can't face, it was a head tilt, half smile, half question kind of facial expression. They all understood what it meant.

'Look, all I can say is that if she had self - harmed or had those thoughts, then of course I would have reported that information immediately to the correct agencies.' answered Jules.

'Okay Jules, if it's okay with you, can you just tell us, what guided visualisation entails and how a trauma tapestry programme works please?' asked Stacey, smiling.

'Well, guided imagery can quickly calm the body down and simultaneously relax a client's mind. It's good for the young ones because it's relaxing and teaches them to calm themselves down internally. To stop a racing brain if you know what I mean? It isn't invasive in any way and they only have to talk about what they are seeing or feeling if they want to.

It is a very quick intervention for de-stressing and a uscful strategy for maintaining resilience toward stress during difficult times. I think Glynis will benefit from its effects for a long time and hopefully, she will continue to use the techniques that she has learned.' replied Jules

'Ah, but I'm still not sure how it works?' asked Rocco.

'Okay, look. It's a bit like having a story read to you, a simple relaxation technique that can help a client quickly and easily calm down. It's virtually as easy as indulging in a vivid daydream and, with practice, the technique can help clients to make sense of their world. A bit like looking down on their life, from a drone perspective.

Then when they come back from their imaginative place or childhood or wherever they have chosen to go, they often have new sense of self, a realisation if you like.' replied Jules.

'And did Glynis have a new sense of self, was she any different do you think, after the session I mean?' asked Rocco.

'She is progressing all the time and her confidence presents far higher than when I first met her, if that's what you mean inspector?' answered Jules.

'So, what exactly is the Trauma Tapestry Programme Jules, it sounds interesting?' asked Rocco.

'It's a unique set of session work that is completed very much outside of the session. First of all the therapist has to find out if the client is any good at or enjoys drawing. It just so happens that Glynis does and is very good at it.'

'Would we be able to see her drawings do you think?' asked Rocco tentatively.

‘I’m afraid not, not at this stage. So, the tapestry is not a quick fix, there is no time limit to the work that can go into it. It works really well with children and teenagers because they are already doing similar work at school, albeit in the name of lessons. Then it is suggested to the client that he/she starts to draw images of their life as they see it from birth to where they are now in life. I encourage them to draw, write letters, songs or poems. Then they bring what they have created to subsequent sessions.

My job as the therapist is to tape the work together under the instruction of the client. Sometimes they want to do this bit themselves, and that's okay too.' continued Jules.

'What do they do once they are all taped together?' asked Stacey.

'Well, if the client is happy to continue with the drawings and to bring them in to each session. The therapist goes through a kind of exploration of what they have presented, colours, textures, you know. That in itself, brings out a whole new set of information that the client may need to talk about.' said Jules.

'Then what do they do with it, I mean it could become huge right?' said Rocco.

'Well, ladies! This is the best bit. Once the client is sure they have all they need within their tapestry, they take it away and burn it, making sure that they keep the ashes. They then choose what they want to do with the ashes. It can be something beautiful, like burying them and planting a tree or scattering them at a significant place from a certain memory in their life.' answered Jules.

'Ah okay, I get it, it's like a catharsis type of exercise. Write it out, let it flow kind of thing?' asked Stacey.

'Yes, if that's how you see it, yes.' answered Jules.

'We may need to have your notes and any art work subpoenaed to the court Jules, when and if any evidence is found to prove Glynis's story. Is that going to be a problem for you?'

'No, not at all, anything that will help that girl is considered as far as I'm concerned. You have my word.'

'Okay Jules, that's all we wanted to hear today, thank you for your time. We'll be in touch if we need to, otherwise we'll see you in court, as they say.' laughed Rocco as they all got up and Jules saw them to the door of the clinic.

Chapter

44

Within just four days, under the authoritative gaze of Trenchie, Rocco had instructed the forensic pathology team to dig up and explore underneath part of the double garage at a previously unsuspecting Mr and Mrs Hilliard's home.

Piece by piece officers helped move the contents of the garage into the Hilliard's conservatory. A concrete breaker was brought in to carefully remove the flooring, layer by layer.

Once they were down to the soil, Chink the force cadaver dog was bought in to trace any decomposition, locate body parts, tissue, blood or bone.

He soon signalled, getting very excited, wagging his tail and barking at a spot in the earth.

Holding him back Gerry, one of the excavators, dug and moved the soil gently away as a small skeletal finger of a left hand was revealed.

As the forensic archaeologists continued to search, they found a complete set of female human remains, the head of which, had been detached.

They carefully collected and tested every scrap of evidence. Proof that this young mother had lived. There was evidence of her clothing, some parts still intact, even the small metal rivets from her jeans were found.

The police photographer, Moira was on hand, taking extensive photographs. She knew her job inside and out and insisted that the two standby cops were wearing their body cameras, filming her and the recovery of the remains every second.

The teams laid out the body, they were able to put together an exact body state and evidence of how Marilyn had died.

The sketches and diagrams provided the best possible evidence for the next stage of the court case. There had been meticulous evidence recovery, bespoke forensic analysis and expert interpretation from some of the UK's most experienced forensic scientists had assisted with this. They all worked through the night until every single piece of the authentic Marilyn Gwen Phelan was located, bagged, tagged and put into a large forensic cool box.

The evidence was laid bare. The remains found at 37 Church View, were indeed a perfect DNA match of the sample that Glynis had given and were found to be beyond doubt, belonging to Marilyn Solomon, nee Phelan.

Chapter 45

The Court was re-established. Rocco was called to give her evidence of what had happened and the events that had led to the present situation with Ms Glynis Solomon.

Once the courtroom was settled, the Judge, Justice Tanya Parkes QC, held up her hand and said.

'This is a particularly emotional case and I ask that as much as possible you try to keep to the facts. Carry on DCI Raven.'

'Thank you your honour. I will read out the findings of this case to date.

'It has been proved that the evidence given by Glynis Louise Solomon on the 25th May 2019 during a court hearing for her, is the complete truth. These are the facts before me.

At just over two years old, Glynis witnessed the murder of her mother, Marilyn Solomon, nee Phelan.

This was perpetrated by her father Mr Raymond Solomon, now deceased. With him at the time was his new girlfriend, Ms Patricia Betts.

Glynis watched them in the garden as they buried the headless corpse alongside the decapitated head of her mother, in a shallow grave. It wasn't long before Raymond Solomon laid a concrete plinth on that piece of garden and built a garage for his classic car.

Because Patricia had a similar resemblance to Marilyn Solomon, nobody was any the wiser. From early social service reports, Patricia claimed the child as her own, using her as a punch bag when the need took her. The child was neglected, at times suffered from malnutrition and kept at home to slave after Patricia whilst Raymond Solomon worked away from the home for long periods of time.'

'Thank you DCI Raven, please take a seat while we call the next statement.' said Justice Tanya Parkes QC.

The clerk to the court called upon Glynis Solomon to read out her personal statement.

Standing in the dock, Glynis took a deep breath and smiled nervously at the Judge, who smiled back and nodded for her to read out her statement.

"When I was about two and a half years old, my father killed my mother, he was with his girlfriend who called herself Marilyn, who you have all been led to believe, is my mother. She is not, she is actually a woman called Patricia Betts.

My father cut my mother's head off with the end of a shovel, they were drunk and giggling as they buried her out the back of the house. I know this because I was watching from the bedroom window. I kept waiting for my mummy to come out of the ground but she never came. I really didn't understand any of it.

That woman Patricia, told me it was my fault that things had changed between us, but I never understood what had happened. She used to drink whiskey all the time and make me drink it too, before she beat me with her hand and sometimes one of my dad's belts.

My eyes and my mind were confused because I know what I saw. I just thought that my mother had changed and it must have been my fault. I guess I hung on to that, because that way, if I did everything right, she might just start being loving and funny again.

Two or three days later, my father laid a concrete base down over where they'd buried her, he built a garage and kept his classic car in there. I spent every moment I could in that garage because I must have felt close to her in there. I now realise why I wanted to be there, in that place. As I close my eyes now, I can see us doing sticking felt pictures.

I had forgotten, but there was a double swing, you know, like a love seat, where the garage had been built. It's as if my body remembered that spot but my mind didn't understand. It is now a clear memory of my mum and how she used to make us laugh all the time."

The silence was deafening in the courtroom as Glynis continued with a shaky little voice.

"My life so far, has really been one of self-destruct. I suppose I started to act out a bit. I was always off from school because that woman, Patricia, kept me at home to clean the house and to fetch and carry for her. Luckily for me, a truancy officer found me and still supports me to this day. I had my first drink and cigarette at about ten years old and by the age of eleven I was being groomed and abused by a group of adult men.

I met a boy, he was older than me, he seemed to like me. I started doing what he wanted because I thought he loved me and I wanted to please him so that he kept on loving me. I got into trouble and started running away from the children's home that I had been put into.

This boy talked me into helping him, he said that all I had to do was go to a party and be nice to the men there. He said it would get him out of trouble and then we could be together properly.

At the 'party' I got seriously sexually assaulted along with some other girls and we somehow manged to run away from them and eventually get ourselves back to the home and try and get on with our lives.

Because everyone around me who was trying to help me, thought I was rebelling against the treatment from my mother, they kind of looked out for me.

I barely spoke to anyone. It was easier not to speak because I had so much confusion going on in my head.

I kept seeing images in my mind of another woman, she was kind and loving. I now realise this was my real mother. From that day, I experienced disturbing and severe flashbacks. I hated these images because they started to confuse me even more. The hatred I had started to feel towards Patricia grew inside me but I didn't really know why. I needed answers but wasn't sure how to get them.

Janette, the social worker who helped me and pretty much saved me, got me some counselling through the children's home. It was the first time I felt able to talk about me and not be judged, told off or given advice.

It was during one of these sessions that I was able to relax and think back, sort of rewind my life and go back to my earlier childhood. Jules, the counsellor asked me to relax and took my mind back to as far back as I could remember. I saw everything as clear as day but I didn't tell her that. I didn't tell anyone until coming to court the first time. It took me weeks to try and sort the images out in my mind, to make sense of the truth. The counsellor and my friend kept asking me what was wrong, but I couldn't tell them because I didn't want them to have those images too."

Tears gently trickled down Glynis's face, but she bravely carried on.

"The boys had given us drugs and I was afraid that I was hallucinating from some kind of after effect. I needed to know what was true and what was false.

I made up my mind that I would go and see Patricia and find out the truth. Janette helped me to find her. She took me to the place where she was living. I swear, I only wanted to talk with her, nothing else.

I wanted to ask her if what I had seen was the truth. And I can tell you all now, that by the look on her face when she saw me, that if she hated me when I was a child, she definitely hated me even more on that day. I didn't need to ask her anything. I knew she wasn't my mother and what I had seen in the counselling session had been real.

I was just a frightened kid who I now know had started to suffer the effects of complex grief and the profound loss of her mother.

Jules taught me a lot and helped me to understand many of my self-soothing behaviours. I had become addicted to digging up graves, I was looking for comfort, like a feeling of love I suppose. Being in a graveyard, in peace and quiet, away from the madness, gave me peace and I felt love. Real love, I liked that feeling. I hadn't felt it in such a long time. It gave me an escape from the real world or from whatever thoughts and feelings I was trying to grasp.

Even now, I am only starting to come to terms with the grief and loss that I feel for my beautiful mum.

And here I am today, here in front of you. Telling you my story. Because people around me have cared enough to help and support me. I have changed beyond recognition and have truly got myself together.

Because of the work I did with Jules, I can start to have space in my head for the beautiful, funny, happy and loving memories of my real mother. Since I told the court about what happened, I've been able to tell Jules the whole truth about what happened when we did the visualisation session.

She has explained to me that I am free now, I am finally allowed to acknowledge that my mum actually existed as a person and not just in my imagination.

I am allowed to recognise and accept the day and date that she was killed. My grief is healthier and I can express it when I need to without being shamed, closed down or behaving in ways that others may see as weird. I didn't have much time with her, but what I did have was real and beautiful.

Thank you for listening to me. Finally.

Glynis Solomon.

The court stayed silent for at least two full minutes as people wiped their faces and regained their composures. Glynis was helped down from the witness box by a court clerk.

'We will now break for lunch and return at fourteen hundred hours for summing up, please do not be late.'

said Justice Tanya Parkes QC, wiping her own tears away.

The court was emptied within thirty minutes as those involved, made their way out to various cafes and to find some refreshments.

Janette and Layla both took turns in hugging Glynis, telling her how brave she had been throughout the whole morning.

‘I’m starving, can we go and get a burger or something?’ replied Glynis, smiling at them both.

‘Come on, I’ll take you, we’ll go through the drive in.’ said Janette, happy to see this young lady still smiling after everything she had just been through.

Chapter 46

Ruth was keeping an eye on the court case from the office by text messages with Mags. From the information that Mags had already given her, she had manged to locate a birth brother and sister of the real Marilyn Solomon, nee Phelan.

Kieran Phelan lived in Bradford and his sister Catherine, whose married name was Noakes, lived not too far from Callachen itself, in a village called Esmond.

On the authorisation of Rocco, Ruth arranged for two officers to call to both siblings immediately to deliver the death message before the news was in the headlines, which no doubt, would be on television that very evening.

Chapter

47

The court re convened as everyone waited silently for the next statements to be read out.

This case was unique in that the Judge had specifically asked for statements to be read out in person, rather than the witnesses and the accused, questioned.

After the coroner, the lead forensic examiner and social services safeguarding manager had read out their statements, both solicitors, prosecuting and defence were asked if they would like to add anything. Both denied, shaking their heads forlornly.

The energy in the courtroom was a combination of electrically charged anticipation and complete and utter empathic compassion for this young girl, who had basically coped somehow, in a silent agony.

Before the jury were asked to leave to consider their verdict, the Judge stood up as she said.

'Members of the Jury and those who have appeared in court today. I don't think we need to hear anymore statements. It is my summing up and conclusion that Ms Solomon has lived her young life in a state of fear and hypervigilance to date. This is primarily due to witnessing the death of her mother as a small child. No child should have to go through such horror, nor should abuse, exploitation and neglect be part of a child's life. I do not consider that there is any cause for concern or that Ms Solomon should be convicted of any crime here. Please take your time to review the facts carefully with the evidence that you have heard today. We will adjourn until you are ready to return with your verdict.'

In the waiting area, Glynis paced the room. Layla tapped her feet relentlessly and Janette was almost rocking with unknown expectation as they waited to be called back into the court.

Rocco and Mags came to the witness room to tell them that Patricia Betts had been arrested for aiding and abetting to murder as well as child cruelty and a few other offences to be taken into consideration.

'Hey, hang on a minute they're calling us back in.' said Rocco suddenly.

'Right come on girls, are you ready? answered Janette.

Glynis was led to the witness box and asked to stand.

The spokesperson for the Jury stood up as the Judge asked.

‘Members of the jury, have you all reached a verdict on which you agree?’

‘Yes your honour.’

‘Please tell us whether you find the defendant guilty or not guilty of the charges bought before this court today?’

‘Not guilty.’ replied the spokesperson.

Glynis smiled and waited for the judge to speak.

‘Well, Ms Solomon, you are free to go, but before you do. I just want to say that I personally am in awe of you my dear. You are one of the bravest people to have ever stood in this court. To speak your truth as seriously and with such honesty for one so young is commendable. Take care of yourself won’t you.’ said the Judge with a smile and a head tilted nod.

The clerk again helped Glynis step down from the witness box and Layla ran to her. They hugged and squealed and hurried out of the court. Janette crossed every boundary in her role and hugged them both again before getting into her car to return to the safe house.

Rocco, Mark, Mags and Stacey were waiting in their cars they all returned to the safe house, Melanie greeted them all at the door.

‘Hi, come on in there are some people here that you might want to meet Glynis?’

Layla looked puzzled at Glynis as they were led into the dining room. Glynis nearly collapsed, she thought it was her mother, the mother she used to know. Melanie introduced Catherine (Kat) as her mother's sister.

'You look so much like her.' said Glynis in disbelief.

'I know I do, everyone used to say that when we were children. You are beautiful Glynis, we have so much to talk about.

This is your uncle Kieran, mine and your mums brother. I have three children and Kieran has two, so you have five cousins as well.'

Kieran held his arms out to Glynis and Kat, the three of them shared a group hug.

'I don't know what to say, I've suddenly gone from having no family to now having seven new real blood relations in my life. This is brilliant.' said Glynis, beaming.

'The thing is Glynis, what are you going to do with your life now that you know you have us?' asked Kieran.

'I'm not sure, I don't think I want to live away from around here. I'm thinking of going on holiday with Layla for the summer, just to give myself some time, you know?' said Glynis.

'Here's my number and here's Kieran's okay, we had no idea that Maz had died, we all fell out years ago over something stupid to do with your dad. I wish now that we had tried to make it up. We would have known in an instant that the other woman was an imposter.' said Kat.

'What about your dad, will you stay with him now do you think?'

'He's dead, he killed himself a few months back, he was useless anyway.' said Glynis, trying to hold back her sadness.

'Oh sorry Glynis, we didn't know that.' answered Kat.

'Look, we just wanted to meet you and to let you know that we are and always will be there for you, should you ever need us. You have our contact details now, so please keep in touch, whatever you decide to do okay?' said Kieran gently.

'We'll leave you to it okay, give you some time to adjust?' added Kat.

'Thank you for coming, I mean it, thank you. After the court case today, it's really made my day. And I will get in touch once I know what's happening.' answered Glynis.

Kieran and Kat left the safe house, Glynis went to her bedroom to lay out on her bed. As usual Layla wasn't far behind her.

'Are you okay?' asked Layla.

'I'm just a bit tired, but I'm happy at the way it's all turned out. replied Glynis, smiling at her friend.

‘I bet you are, after the morning you’ve had! I’ve sorted everything out with Janette and she has authorised it all for tomorrow as planned. Are you ready? asked Layla, looking at her friend.

‘I’m ready!’ replied Glynis.

Chapter

48

When the plane touched down, the heat hit Glynis instantly, she had never known anything like it, she loved it and the way it made her skin feel. It was a comforting, warm dry heat.

A very tanned, middle aged man held a name board up with the words Layla Anderson.

'Hi, I'm Oliver Jensen, I've been waiting for you to arrive. As you know by now, I am the solicitor who is dealing with your mothers case and your new home. I'm here to take you there and to go through the documents with you. We obviously don't have to do that today.' he said smiling.

'Oh okay thanks, will you just take us to the house and let us get settled first, I can come and find you tomorrow, when we've slept.' said Layla.

'Of course, let's go and show you your new place shall we?' said Oliver as he opened a car door for each of them.

Oliver helped them in to the house with their luggage. The house was enormous, the rooms were huge and it was immaculately decorated. They chose their bedrooms and decided that they needed to go and get some food in before settling in for the evening.

'Have you got the bank card and account details Glynis.' asked Layla quietly.

'Yes they're safely inside one of my socks.' replied Glynis laughing.

'Okay girls, here are your keys for the house, I'll show you how everything works and then if you like, I'll take you to the supermarket. You would be better off to get it delivered after this first time, seeing as neither of you are old enough to drive.' said Oliver.

'Okay let's look at what we need then.' said Layla as she looked through the cupboards.

'There's five hundred dollars here in this cupboard, keep it locked. It's pretty safe around here but you never know. You can use it for the next few weeks for shopping and the like. I've arranged for your allocated legal guardian to visit tomorrow so that you have constant access to her and you will know what is and isn't authorised, she will be able to organise prison visits and will have all details of your new school and what you will need to do to start at the end of the summer.

Your mother has left everything in place and I am in touch with Janette your safeguarding social worker, from England. You know the score if you fall off of the programme, you'll go right back to blighty.' smiled Oliver.

Shopping in Australia was an experience, the shop workers all wore roller skates, it looked like fun, they both commented to Oliver.

After a long shop and two hundred dollars later, laden with food and toiletries. They transferred the bags into the house, all of them attempting to find the right places to put everything away.

'I'll leave you to it then ladies. You have my number, now take care and I'll see you in a couple of days to sort the paperwork out.' said Oliver.

'Okay, thanks so much for your help, see you soon.' replied Layla as she saw him out of the door.

'Bloody hell Layla, he went on a bit didn't he?' said Glynis.

'Come on, let's get some food, I'm starving.' replied Layla.

Chapter

49

‘Do you think they’ll be alright Rocco?’ asked Stacey.

‘Yes, it was all sorted for them, being part of the witness protection scheme got all their boxes ticked more quickly. The fact that Layla’s mother already has Australian citizenship will help them both to work towards getting their own. Yeah, I think they’ll be alright, I really do.’ replied Rocco.

‘Are you and Mark having a thing?’ asked Stacey.

Rocco spat her coffee out all over her lap in the police car.

‘You pick your moments don’t you?’ answered Rocco, laughing.

‘I was just wondering, that’s all. You know, after the phone call when he answered your phone and said you’d left it in his car. You’ve never ever left your phone anywhere Roc! He’s a nice bloke, you could do worse you know?’ continued Stacey.

Rocco kept her cool and her own counsel as she drank what was left of her coffee.

'I suppose it's all around the office by now then is it?' asked Rocco.

'Yes it is boss, yes it is.' said Stacey, smiling at her.

A call came in on the radio, Stacey turned the volume up to listen.

Child abduction in Callachen market. Taken from its pushchair while the father was buying some vegetables.

'We had better go, put your foot down Stacey.' said Rocco.

Book 1

The Salvaging of Sonny Chapman is the first of three novellas telling the story of a young mother from Derbyshire, England. Sonny works as a portrait artist, commissioned by the bereaved relatives of those whose loved ones have died. As Sonny sketches the eyes of the portraits she works on, she starts to hear their voices, just as if she is having a conversation with them.

Book 2

The Restoration of Sonny Chapman is the second book in the trilogy. Sonny's life has changed from violent chaos and her very near death, to a more peaceful and safe place. In the stunning setting of her new husbands birthplace. The beautiful ancient backdrop of Tuscany, Italy, where his world and family have entwined with hers. Thinking that she has left her psychic ability behind, she begins to reconnect with those who have passed over.

Available from Amazon Online and all

Major High Street Book stores

suejdaniels.com
stonefacepublishingaudio.com

Book 3

The Journals of Sonny Chapman is the third, and final, book in the trilogy. Now, with three full journals in the family, Mirabella, wise beyond her years, sets up her own room in the Cat's Eye Clinic. She starts to feel danger and senses the energy of a woman who abducted her as a child. Nightmares take her to the edge of madness as the contents of three journals are sought after by a new and vicious enemy.

DCI Rochelle Raven Series

The Cubby Hole; Holly Knowles had always been afraid of the dark, even as a baby she would cry incessantly until her parents started to realise that by leaving a small 'plug in' baby lamp on, they could get a good five or six hours sleep before she woke up. The Galaxy Unit was relatively new to the force, it had been set up two years previously, specifically to work with cases of child abduction and murder.

DCI Rochelle Raven Series

Glynis; Glynis Solomon came from a long line of angry, broken females. She had fought every day of her young life, to survive the regular outbursts of her violent, whiskey drinking, alcoholic mother. Barely coping psychologically as she was dragged through the social care system, confused and afraid as her silent rage simmered. She kept herself tightly, like a coiled spring, observing all around her but never speaking.

Available from Amazon Online and all

Major High Street Book stores

suejdaniels.com
stonefacepublishingaudio.com

DCI Rochelle Raven Series

Stella; Stella is the child of Polish Parents, Marta and Jakob Lonski. Taken without warning at the age of just two years old from her pushchair, whilst her father, leaving her for a second or two to buy fruit from a local market. Her family never stop looking for her, in fact, they make it their personal crusade to find her.

Available from Amazon Online and all

Major High Street Book stores

suejdaniels.com
stonefacepublishingaudio.com